W9-BUX-712

More Critical Praise for Elizabeth Nunez

for *Even in Paradise*

"*King Lear* in the Caribbean—except in this novel, the flattery and deceit of Glynis (Goneril) and Rebecca (Regan) lose out to the principled, honest love of their younger sister, Corinne (Cordelia)."
—*O, the Oprah Magazine*, "21 Books to Read This May"

"[A]n epic tale of family betrayal and manipulation couched in superbly engaging prose and peopled with deftly drawn characters. In a story structure as rhythmic as the ebb and flow of the water surrounding Trinidad and Barbados, this revisiting of the classic story of King Lear becomes a subtle, organic exploration of politics, class, race, and privilege. A dazzling, epic triumph."   —*Kirkus Reviews*, starred review

for *Not for Everyday Use*

• Winner of the 2015 Hurston/Wright Legacy Award in Nonfiction
• Long-listed for the 2015 OCM Bocas Prize in Nonfiction

"Nunez ponders the cultural, racial, familial, social, and personal experiences that led to what she ultimately understands was a deeply loving union between her parents. A beautifully written exploration of the complexities of marriage and family life."   —*Booklist*, starred review

"Through her thoughtful and articulate writing, Nunez offers a valuable perspective on the racism that she experienced, even in America, and the damage the Catholic Church does to women who follow the 'no artificial birth control' rule. Recommended for memoir enthusiasts and readers interested in Caribbean literature."   —*Library Journal*

"A narrative that feels like a close friend talking about her past . . . An insightful, generous story."   —*Oprah.com*

for *Boundaries*

• A finalist for the 2012 NAACP Image Award in Literature

"Many moments of elegant, overarching insight bind the personal to the collective past." —*New York Times Book Review*, Editors' Choice

"Nunez deftly dissects the immigrant experience in light of cultural traditions that impact family roles, professional obligations, and romantic opportunities."   —*Booklist*

"Elizabeth Nunez is one of the finest and most necessary voices in contemporary American and Caribbean fiction."
                        —Colum McCann, author of *Let the Great World Spin*

"A quiet, sensitive portrait . . . This work covers a lot of ground, from mother-daughter and male-female relationships to the tensions between immigrants and the American born."   —*Library Journal*

for *Anna In-Between*

• Winner of the 2010 PEN Oakland Josephine Miles Award
• Long-listed for the 2011 IMPAC Dublin Literary Award

"A psychologically and emotionally astute family portrait, with dark themes like racism, cancer, and the bittersweet longing of the immigrant."
                        —*New York Times Book Review*, Editors' Choice

"Nunez has created a moving and insightful character study while delving into the complexities of identity politics. Highly recommended."
                        —*Library Journal*, starred review

"Nunez deftly explores family strife and immigrant identity in her vivid latest . . . with expressive prose and convincing characters that immediately hook the reader."   —*Publishers Weekly*, starred review

for *Prospero's Daughter*

"The very title of Elizabeth Nunez's gripping and richly imagined sixth novel, *Prospero's Daughter*, distances her work from both the original *Tempest* (in which the daughter, Miranda, is perhaps the least developed of all Shakespearean heroines) and from the many postcolonial reactions to the play . . . Nunez, who is a master at pacing and plotting, explores the motivations behind Caliban's outburst, hatching an entirely new story that is inspired by Shakespeare, but not beholden to him."
                        —*New York Times Book Review*

Also by Elizabeth Nunez

NOW

LILA

KNOWS

elizabeth nunez

BROOKLYN, NEW YORK

Published by Akashic Books
©2022 Elizabeth Nunez

Hardcover ISBN: 978-1-63614-024-7
Library of Congress Control Number: 2021945692

Akashic Books
Instagram: AkashicBooks
Twitter: AkashicBooks
Facebook: AkashicBooks
E-mail: info@akashicbooks.com
Website: www.akashicbooks.com

We must always take sides. Neutrality helps the oppressor, never the victim. Silence encourages the tormentor, never the tormented. Sometimes we must interfere.

—Elie Wiesel

The ultimate tragedy is not the oppression and cruelty by the bad people but the silence over that by the good people.

—Dr. Martin Luther King Jr.

For my granddaughter Savannah Nunez Harrell who knows

1

On the day Lila Bonnard arrived in America to begin teaching at Mayfield College, named for the eponymous small town in a bucolic area of Vermont, there was a killing. Some said it was an accidental killing. They claimed that the man who lay on the sidewalk of Main Street bleeding from gunshot wounds to his head and chest just happened to be in the wrong place at the wrong time. The few who knew the secrets the man held in his heart disagreed: the dead man was in the right place at the right time; it was his reason for being there that was wrong. But there were other people, though only three, who eschewed all excuses and explanations. The man was murdered in cold blood, they said. There could be no other way to spin his senseless death.

The taxi that was bringing Lila from the airport to the home of Mrs. Lowell, where Dr. Campbell, the chair of the English department, had arranged for Lila to stay during the year of her appointment as visiting professor at Mayfield, had been forced to pull aside when a line of police cars and two ambulances screeched past them, sirens blasting, red and blue strobe lights sending violent bright slashes across the elegant barrels brimming over with late-summer flowers that dotted the sidewalks of Main Street. "Must have used all the ambulances in

the town," the driver said to Lila when a police officer stopped him from going farther. "Somebody must
be dead for sure. Never saw nothing like this. May take
some time, but I can wait."

"How much time?" Lila asked.

"Dunno. Never saw nothing like this," he repeated.
"Must be five cars waiting in front of us, and more than
a dozen behind."

Lila looked out the car window. An elderly couple had stopped a group of middle-aged women who
said something to them, shook their heads, and left the
couple standing on the sidewalk, the elderly woman's
hand clasped to her mouth in shock, the man tightening
his grasp on her arm. Some young people ran past the
women—students, Lila assumed, for two of them wore
sweatshirts with a huge M emblazoned on the back. The
cabdriver stuck his head out of the window and called
to them: "What's happening?"

"Professor in trouble," one of the young women said.

"Professor from Mayfield?"

"You know another college here?" her male companion shot back as he raced with her down the street.

"Think they are hotshots," the driver said, turning
back to Lila. "The whole lot of them think they're better
than us who live here all our lives. Sure, I know Mayfield
is the only college in town. Must be something the professor did. In trouble, that girl said."

"How much farther?" Lila asked.

"Farther where?"

"To where I'm going."

"'Bout another four blocks. Two blocks down Main
Street and then turn right, two more blocks and you'll

be there. Looks like it'll be a while before I can move. I can wait, but I have to keep the meter running. It'll cost you."

"I can walk four blocks," Lila said.

"With your luggage?"

"If you'll take it out of the boot for me."

"Boot?"

"Trunk. I have only one suitcase."

The cabdriver shrugged. "Suit yourself," he said, and he walked around to the back of the cab, took out Lila's suitcase, and placed it on the sidewalk. He barely looked at her when she paid him and mumbled a garbled thank you when she added a tip.

He had been distinctly rude to her. *Suit yourself*. It hadn't suited him when the taxi dispatcher at the airport directed her to get in his cab. It hadn't suited him either when the dispatcher barked at him to put her suitcase in the trunk: "You going to sit there and leave the girl standing on the sidewalk with her luggage?" He had reluctantly got out of the cab to take her luggage, but once back at the wheel, after brusquely asking for the address where he was to drive her, his next question was just as gruff: "Where're you from?"

She said the Caribbean and he didn't ask for more, from which island, and so she didn't see the need to tell him more. He was silent for a while, and then, as if he had been pondering the question, he asked, "Going back?"

"I'm here only for a year," she said.

His shoulders relaxed. "One year. Good." His mood changed; he was practically smiling. He switched on the radio. Country music. He began humming. "Do you mind?" he asked.

"'Kiss an Angel Good Morning,' Charlie Pride," she offered.

"You know him?" And then he added brightly, "I guess you would."

Lila knew what he meant: Charlie Pride was Black. But she also knew and loved other country music singers—Johnny Cash, Willie Nelson, Dolly Parton, Reba McEntire, Patsy Cline. She could sing their songs by heart.

Was it so obvious she wasn't American? White American, that is? Back on her island most people would not have been so ready to make the assumption that she would prefer Charlie Pride because African blood ran through her veins. Other bloods ran in her veins too, bloods from European ancestors. She was fair-skinned; her complexion not so light that she would be mistaken for white, but they wouldn't say she was Black either. Café au lait would be an apt description. Robert, her fiancé, who was still on the island she left that morning, preferred caramel. He said she was the color of the candy and just as sweet. She was attractive, he declared, and though she would admit that when she was in the bloom of her youth she had been pretty, at thirty-three her prettiness was already beginning to fade. Her jet-black hair was no longer as thick as it once was and she had cut it short, to the disappointment of her friends who thought she was fortunate that she had not had to use weaves to extend the length. But the soft ringlets close to her head sharpened the slopes of her cheeks, the brightness of her eyes, and the contours of her heart-shaped lips. Robert said she would seem exotic to Americans. "Watch if one of them won't fall in love with you."

She had wasted no time in reassuring him: "You are the love of my life."

But it seemed the cabdriver *had* noticed her looks. As she was making her way down the street, her arms aching from pulling her suitcase, her handbag, and small duffel bag cutting into her shoulder, he shouted after her, "A good-looking girl like you needs to be careful. There's trouble down there!"

Down there was much farther than the two blocks she had to walk before turning off to the street that led to the house where she was going to stay, and as uneasy as she was, Lila figured it was enough of a distance from the trouble for her to be safe. But she got caught in the swell of students rushing past her and bumping into her on all sides, and before she knew it she had passed her turn. Another wave came, followed by another and another, each larger and stronger, the students shouting and yelling excitedly. *Professor, woman, police*—those were the few words she could discern through the roar of their voices and the thunderous pounding of hard soles against the concrete. They pushed her so violently from the back that she was carried forward, her feet involuntarily increasing her pace though the muscles in her arms ached and she wished nothing more than to stop and catch her breath.

The police were shouting orders now from a bullhorn: "*Move back! Move back!*" Then the eerie ricocheting of firecrackers. "Gunshots!" someone yelled. And just as swiftly and powerfully as they had pushed her forward, the waves retreated, the students elbowing each other in their desperate haste to save themselves from an errant bullet. The force of their retreat was so powerful that Lila was thrown down to her knees.

A space opened up then and Lila saw it; she witnessed it: the trouble. And though she did not know it at the time, what she witnessed would make demands on her that nothing in her past experiences on her Caribbean island had prepared her to understand or to address.

2

The students were not wrong: a professor was in trouble. Lila did not know him, could not know him; she had just arrived at Mayfield. But she was certain the man astride a woman lying on the sidewalk was indeed a professor when she heard a female voice shout out to the police: "Don't hurt him! It's Dr. Brown, he teaches at the college."

The remarkable thing was that the man was Black and the woman who lay beneath him was white. Perhaps the difference in their skin color would not have been as remarkable if she had seen such a man and such a woman in such a dangerously suggestive position on the sidewalk of the main street in her hometown. She would have been alarmed, of course. What would have alarmed her would not have been their color but the state of the woman, her face bloodless, almost as pale and gray as the sun-bleached concrete she lay on. But Lila was not in the Caribbean where most of the men and women were dark-skinned, and where people of mixed ethnicities were not uncommon. From the moment the taxi driver had turned out of the airport, however, she had not seen a single person of color, not brown, not Black, not Asian. Nothing changed as they entered the town of Mayfield. Like the taxi driver, the people there were all the same—all of them white, the students too who had rushed past her and again away from her. So what she noticed first, and what was remarkable to her, was that the man, the professor, was Black. And what startled her even more was that the woman trying to come to his aid, the woman begging the police not to hurt him, was Black too.

Two police cars had joined the three others that had screeched down the street behind the flashing lights of the ambulance. Sirens still blasting, the police officers jumped out of their cars, their hands clasped to the guns on their hips, and began pushing back the few students and townspeople who, in spite of the orders from the police, were still hovering nearby.

"Move out! Move out!" the officers shouted. Everyone backed away, some so quickly they stumbled upon each other.

"Don't hurt him!" the Black woman yelled again. "I know him, I tell you. I can vouch for him."

Lila was petrified; she could not move. From where she was, hunkered down on her knees, she could see three policemen, their guns drawn, sprinting toward the area where the man was still astride the woman on the sidewalk.

The policeman holding the bullhorn raised it to his mouth. "Get off her!" he shouted to the man. "Get up! Now!"

"Stop!" the Black woman screamed again. "He's helping her! Stop!"

"Stay back!" the officer yelled at her.

"It's Ron. Dr. Brown. He teaches at the college," the woman pleaded.

"Stay back, I'm warning you. Stay back!" the officer yelled again.

"He's helping—"

"I'm warning you. I won't warn you again."

The officer with the bullhorn was now crouched behind another officer who was just a few feet from the man. "Take your hands off her!" he yelled. "Move away! Now!"

"Ron, do as he says! Leave her," the woman begged the man.

Two more officers approached the sidewalk and now there were four of them close to the man, their guns drawn. One of them, his finger on the trigger of his gun, shouted to his partner: "Make that woman go back!" He was standing with his feet apart, arms extended, gun raised, pointed forward.

"Don't shoot him!" the woman screamed. The officer pushed her back into the street.

Instinctively, heedless of the danger to herself, Lila rose from her knees to help the woman who was struggling to steady herself on her feet. "Go back," the woman whispered hoarsely to Lila. "It's not safe to stay here." Her breath came in short, pained spurts.

"Lean on me." Lila put her arm around the woman's waist and helped her walk to the other side of the street, farther up the block. "Sit, sit here." Lila lowered the woman to the curb. "I'll go see. Tell me how I can help."

The woman shook her head. "No. Stay here with me."

But Lila had already removed her arm from around the woman's waist and had stood up. "He may be hurt," she said.

There were tears in the woman's eyes. "Tell Ron to do as the police say. Tell him to move away."

Would he listen to me? Lila felt she had to take that

chance. Perhaps if the man followed the police officer's order, he wouldn't get hurt.

She moved closer. She could see the man clearly now. His legs were straddled across the chest of the woman who was lying prone on the sidewalk. The officer with his finger on the trigger was advancing closer to the man, once more ordering him to step away. "I won't say it again. Get off her!" The officer's voice was trembling slightly. "I say, move away! Put your hands up! Put them up!"

The man lowered his head over the woman's face and fastened his lips to her mouth.

A shot rang out. Then a bloodcurdling scream that seemed to come from the deep well of a woman's heart ripped through the bucolic air of Mayfield Town. Lila did not have to look. She knew who had screamed. "Don't shoot! Please, please don't shoot him," the woman begged the police. Tears rolled down her cheeks. Once again she repeated that the man was a professor. "Please stop!"

Too late.

Four more shots rang out. A man lay sprawled out on the sidewalk, a thin red stream curling down the side of his face from a hole in his head, his white shirt soaked with the deepest of reds from the wounds in his chest, and on Main Street the perfume of late-summer roses and lilacs blended into the metallic scent of blood.

A fog, thick, black, draped over Lila. She heard the sirens, but she did not see when a police officer put the woman in his car, or when the medics ran out of the ambulance with a stretcher. She did not see because when the shots rang out, she sank to the ground, clasped her hands over her ears, and buried her head in her lap.

What she heard next was the gentle voice of a man urging her to get up. He touched her arm lightly. "Here," he said. "Hold on to me. You cannot stay here. Don't be afraid. I won't hurt you."

She looked up into the kindest of eyes, blue as the ocean around her island. He was holding her suitcase and her duffel bag. "I can help you with your handbag too," he said.

She yielded to him with hardly a murmur.

"Where to?" he asked.

And without the slightest hesitation, she gave him her address.

3

He did not stay when they reached the front gate of Mrs. Lowell's house. He had not said a word to her either on the short walk to get there though they walked side by side, she accepting his invitation to slip her arm in the crook of his elbow. Her nerves were still raw and it was a comfort for her to feel his strength. Only after he waved goodbye and was already at the end of the block did she realize that they had not introduced themselves to each other. She did not know his name and neither did he know hers. But he did not seem a stranger to Mayfield and she expected that before long their paths would cross again and she would be able to thank him for his kindness.

Mrs. Lowell's home was an old stately Victorian house, one in a row of similar houses on either side of a tree-lined street. Eaves decorated with white fretwork jutted out from the upper windows. The shingles were painted in a matching palette of pastel colors, the shutters white set against darker pastel-colored window frames, everything pretty as a picture. As she climbed up the steps to the front door, Lila felt she had been thrown back into another century. It was not an unpleasant feeling. Her island had not yet caught up with America's modern buildings of steel and glass. Though it had achieved independence more than half a century ago, the British influence was so woven into the everyday life of the people that they were loath to raze down the old Victorian houses. Indeed, many of the more recent buildings had mounted eaves overhanging the front walls, imitating the bygone days of the English aristocracy. Lila's paternal grandmother lived in an old Victorian house passed down to her by her family. Like the shutters on Mrs. Lowell's house, her grandmother's house was pale gray, the fretwork on the eaves dazzling white.

Lila had just pressed the bell and her finger was poised to press it a second time when the front door opened. A tiny woman, slim as a reed, her wiry frame exacerbated by a bent back which she tried unsuccessfully to straighten, warbled, "Welcome, welcome." Her bony fingers grasped Lila's hand and squeezed it affectionately. "I was worried to death. I was expecting you more than an hour ago. Come in, come in."

Lila had not imagined she would be so old. Dr. Campbell had written that she had arranged for Lila to stay at the home of a longtime friend of her family during her year as visiting professor in the English Department. She explained that the town had only one apartment building which, unfortunately, was fully occupied. Most people either owned their homes or they rented space in someone else's home. Mrs. Lowell lived by herself and had lots of room in her house. Dr. Campbell assured Lila that she would be comfortable there. Lila had assumed that as Mrs. Lowell was a friend of Dr. Campbell's family and lived alone, she would be younger. It was a prejudicial assumption for her own grandmother lived by herself and she was over eighty. Meeting her now, Lila realized that Mrs. Lowell was likely the same age as her grandmother, but her grandmother was not as frail. Perhaps it was the texture of her grandmother's pale, but distinctly brown skin that had resisted the ravages of time; her skin loosened and drooped but it did not wrinkle. Mrs. Lowell was almost alabaster white and her wrinkles cut deep into her paper-thin skin. Her gray eyes were youthful, though. They sparkled when she welcomed Lila into her home and her thin lips widened playfully with a broad smile.

"Your suitcase." Mrs. Lowell stretched out her hand to pick it up. "Let me help you with that."

"No, no," Lila said quickly and kept her hand firmly on the handle of the suitcase. "I can carry it."

"Then the handbag?"

Lila passed it to her. "I'm so sorry to have kept you waiting. There was—"

"I know. I was so worried for you. I heard the sirens. Must have been a bad accident. Dr. Campbell was here. She wanted to welcome you. Then someone from the college called . . ." She looked inquiringly at Lila and when Lila remained silent, she said, "I hope it wasn't one of the students who got in an accident. Last year one of them almost got knocked down when he was crossing the street. The driver was speeding. All those young people speed." Her eyes scanned Lila from top to bottom. "Pretty," she said. Lila lowered her eyes; her face felt warm. She was about to return the compliment when Mrs. Lowell asked abruptly, "Did you hear the sirens?"

Lila mumbled she was glad when the sirens stopped.

"They were so loud. Must have been more than one police car. Was there an ambulance too? The kid must have been really hurt."

Mrs. Lowell was looking directly at her as if waiting for her corroboration. A slight trembling had begun along the woman's lower eyelids. Lila wished at that moment she could tell her she was right. But it was not a student who lay bleeding on the ground.

Mrs. Lowell sighed. "Poor kid. It must have been why Dr. Campbell had to leave in a hurry."

"I hope I get to see Dr. Campbell soon," Lila said.

Mrs. Lowell was still searching her face. "Did you see what happened?"

Lila had no doubt that Dr. Campbell knew the truth. The person who called her from the college must have told her, and if she did not know the details, she knew it was not a student but one of the professors who lay bleeding on the pavement, probably dead. Perhaps Dr. Campbell had allowed Mrs. Lowell to assume it was a student, but Lila was not about to take responsibility for shattering her illusions. So she skirted around the answer. She said the police were there and there was an ambulance, but she did not say more. She said nothing about the gunshots or the man bleeding from his temple or the woman lying next to him. "I expect Dr. Campbell will tell you all about it," she said.

Mrs. Lowell flattened her fingers against her lips and emitted a low hum. It was as if she were trying to push back words traveling up her vocal cords and had finally succeeded in transforming them into a garbled musical note, but she did not press Lila for more. "I suppose Dr. Campbell will call me tonight," she said softly. "She'll give me the details."

"Yes," Lila replied, "Dr. Campbell will know more than I do."

Mrs. Lowell inhaled, breathed out, and released Lila. "And the taxi had no problems bringing you here?"

Lila told her that the police had blocked the road. She had to walk.

"Walk with a heavy suitcase?"

Lila said a man helped her.

Mrs. Lowell didn't seem surprised. "This is a wonderful town. I've lived here all my life. People are kind. Did you get the man's name?"

Lila hadn't; she couldn't even offer a description. The fog that had enveloped her had cleared, but she was not settled inside. A vein still thrummed slightly in her neck. All she could remember were his eyes.

"Never mind," Mrs. Lowell said, waving her hand over her face. "It's a small town. You'll see him again. Come. I'll take you upstairs. I was glad Dr. Campbell arranged for you to stay here. It will be good to have company. Not that I will interfere . . ." She reddened and looked away.

Lila was quick to reassure her: "I was so happy when Dr. Campbell said I could stay with her friend. I am grateful to you for allowing me to come here. My grandmother was worried for me . . ."

"Your grandmother?" Mrs. Lowell's eyes brightened.

"She was afraid for me to be by myself in a strange country. You know, if anything should happen . . ."

"You're close?"

"With my grandmother? Yes," Lila said.

"So you live with her."

"No." Lila smiled. "I wish I could, but she won't allow it. She claimed I wouldn't find a boyfriend if I lived with her."

"And did you? Did you find a boyfriend?"

Normally, Lila would find such a question intrusive. She had just met Mrs. Lowell; objectively they were strangers, but the walls she usually constructed around herself to protect her privacy were falling down.

"I have a fiancé," Lila said.

"And he allowed you to leave him for a year?"

Lila bristled slightly at the notion of "allowed." Her fiancé had not allowed her; she had chosen to leave. "Being invited to come to Mayfield College was too big an opportunity for me to pass up," she said. "I didn't want to miss it. A year is not long. Anyway, it's not for a calendar year; it's for an academic year and there are vacations in between when I plan to go back."

"I missed my husband from the day he died," Mrs. Lowell said. "I miss him now. Every day."

"Oh, I'm sorry. I didn't mean to say it wouldn't be hard being away from Robert. Robert's my fiancé."

Mrs. Lowell's tightened her lips, and she reached into her pocket and pulled out a tissue. "Enough of my jabbering," she said, and dabbed away the moisture that had collected in the well of her eyes. "You must be tired. I better show you where you'll stay."

Lila was relieved. She wasn't ready to talk about Robert. It was enough to say they had agreed that she would accept the offer from Mayfield. But Mrs. Lowell was no fool. She would know that two people in love would not so readily and willingly part from each other even for just an academic year. For true lovers, those nine months would be excruciating.

Mrs. Lowell was already at the staircase. "Take your time coming up behind me," she said. "I know these stairs. They are safe but you are not familiar with them. You tell me your suitcase isn't heavy, but it isn't small either. Why don't you just bring up your duffel bag now and get the suitcase later."

Lila did as Mrs. Lowell recommended and followed her up the stairs. "My room is below yours," Mrs. Lowell said. "You have the second floor to yourself."

It was a substantial space: a large bedroom with windows facing the tree-lined street, another room she could use as an office, and her own bathroom with a shower and bathtub.

"There are blinds you can pull down if it gets too sunny for you," Mrs. Lowell said.

"Where I come from it's sunny most of the time. I love being in a sunny room. I can't thank you enough."

Mrs. Lowell ran her hands down the sides of her dress, her face glowing. "You are welcome to use the other rooms in the house. My bedroom is on the main floor, but you can watch TV in the den."

"I hope with you," Lila said.

"If you don't mind."

"I'd love nothing better."

"I look at the soaps," Mrs. Lowell said. She was practically giggling.

"And I expect the news too."

"Politicians get on my nerves, but I have to keep up. It's my country. I need to know what they are doing."

"Well, I need to know too, so I'm looking forward to having you keep me abreast. What goes on in America affects the world, even my little island. They say when America sneezes, the world catches a cold."

"Sometimes politicians are careless. They don't realize their influence. But do you look at the soaps too, Ms. Bonnard?"

"Lila. You must call me Lila."

"So I will. Lila. It's a lovely name. Reminds me of lilies." Mrs. Lowell did not offer a reciprocal invitation and Lila did not expect one. She would give her the respect due to someone her age.

"It was my mother's favorite flower. She gave me that name. My grandmother objected. She's Catholic. She wanted me to have a saint name."

"What about Lillian?"

"It's the name my grandmother would have chosen."

"And your mother wouldn't have been satisfied with Lillian?"

"I don't know. She died when I was three years old. A car accident. My father was driving. Both of them died."

Mrs. Lowell blinked, her eyes starting to glisten.

"Oh, it was a long, long time ago," Lila said, regretting what she had said.

"But it must have been hard. It would have been hard for me." Mrs. Lowell blinked again.

"My grandmother was mother and father to me," Lila said. "I had a very happy childhood."

"I had no children," Mrs. Lowell said.

"I'm sorry."

"Don't be sorry." The woman brightened. "I had a wonderful husband and I have good friends."

"Dr. Campbell."

"She brought you to me, you see."

"I'll do my best not to disappoint you, Mrs. Lowell."

"How could you? I like you already. But tell me about that grandmother of yours who wanted to name you

Lillian. I take it she was your paternal grandmother, yes?"

"She's very religious."

"I'm a Christian," Mrs. Lowell said. "But I don't belong to any religion. Too many rules I don't want to follow."

If Lila had not already felt a bond with Mrs. Lowell, she felt it intensely now. She too objected to the strictures of religion, especially her grandmother's religion.

"So do you indulge in that foolishness?" Mrs. Lowell asked, and for a second Lila misunderstood the question. As impossible as it seemed, she thought Mrs. Lowell had read her mind. She wrinkled her brow. "I don't always agree. But there are some—"

"Yes, yes, there are some rules that make sense. I can't disagree with that. The Ten Commandments. They keep people from doing bad things to each other. But I was talking about the soaps. Do you look at them, Ms. Bonnard? I mean Lila."

Lila laughed. "My grandmother loves the soaps, especially *General Hospital*. You can't speak to her when *General Hospital* is on."

"Your grandmother is a woman after my own heart."

"You'd like each other," Lila said.

Mrs. Lowell turned toward the door. "Well, I better leave you alone to arrange your things. Take your time going back down for your suitcase."

4

It had been less than two hours since she'd arrived in Vermont and so much had already happened. There had been a killing. The man was dead, Lila was sure of that. Try as she might, Lila could not blot out the image seared into her brain of his blood running in a single tiny rivulet down the side of his face and pooling dark and red on his neck. Four shots she had heard. There might have been more before she buried her head between her legs and her brain shut off all sound.

Mrs. Lowell had calmed her nerves; the throbbing in her neck had subsided completely. She lay down on the bed and stretched out her legs. Her taut muscles loosened and she relaxed. Mrs. Lowell had said Mayfield is a wonderful town. She was safe, in a safe house, on a quiet safe street. Nothing could harm her; there was nothing to worry about.

Unless she remembered.

The woman was alive; *that* she could allow herself to remember. Before the shots rang out, she had seen her lift her hand in the air and call out the man's name. "Ron!" she had said. Then she heard the heavy beat of shoes on the hard asphalt as the police officers ran toward her. One of them shouted, "Do you have it?" The question ricocheted to her.

The gun. Did the police officer have his gun? Was he going to shoot the woman too?

"Naloxone! Quick!" They were the next words she heard as she sank her head down deeper, willing the world to go black.

"Naloxone? She was an addict," Robert said authoritatively. He had picked up the phone on the first ring. "Anything wrong?"

They had spoken already at the airport when she called to let him know she had arrived safely. Now she had called again. She wanted his reassurance. Universities are safe places, Robert would remind her. She'd be protected. It worried her, though, that the dead man was a professor, and so she decided to withhold that part about what she had witnessed on Main Street. Robert would only add it to the list of reasons she should not have accepted the offer from Mayfield. She'd tell him she believed that the man died; she would not say he was a professor, on the faculty of the very college where she would be teaching.

"No, no. I'm fine," she said quickly. "I just wanted to hear your voice."

"You've changed your mind? Is that it? You want to come back? Because if you do . . ."

She stopped him before he could continue: "It's just for a short while, Robert." She had called hoping he would comfort her, and now it was he who needed comforting. "I'll be back soon. You know that."

"A year is not a short while," he said, raising his voice slightly.

"We agreed."

"You decided and I complied."

He was right; she had decided and he agreed because, as he said, he didn't want to lose her.

"It's not going to be easy for me either," she said.

"Then why are you there?"

It was a rabbit hole she didn't want to fall into again. Their quarrels had lasted for weeks. Her grandmother did not approve of their engagement. "You have to choose, Lila," Robert had said. "I'm asking you to spend the rest of your life with me." She argued that Mayfield would give them the time and space to think. He said he didn't need time and space to think. He wanted to marry her now. Her grandmother had made her life, he said. Lila had to make hers.

She said her grandmother had raised her; she could not hurt her. He said—though cautiously—that her grandmother would not have many more years to live. That *they* had decades to be together. That *they* would have children, a family. Their own family.

Ultimately, he had relented. One year, he said.

Now she tried to assuage his anxiety. "I miss you too, Robert."

"You know when you'll be back?"

"It's too soon to be talking about a date. I haven't even met Dr. Campbell."

"So where are you?"

"I'm at Mrs. Lowell's home, where I'll be staying."

"And Dr. Campbell wasn't there to greet you?"

"Something happened and she had to leave," Lila said, and immediately regretted that she had stated it so bluntly.

Robert peppered her with questions and Lila finally

told him what she could: about the police, about the dead man, about the woman lying on the ground next to him.

"Was she dead too?"

Lila said she had seen the woman lift her hands. The police officers rushed to her. One of them asked for naloxone. That was when Robert said, with a cold bitterness in his voice, "She *was* an addict. Don't get mixed up in this, Lila."

5

She had fallen asleep in the clothes she was wearing when she arrived. Birds squabbling over something in the trees outside her window woke her up. She had not drawn the curtains and the shadows of leaves shifting back and forth threw lacy patterns against the thin blinds on the windows. It was already morning. She was still in a daze but she knew where she was. The sunlight was different from the sunlight she had just left on her Caribbean island; the rays there were bright but not piercing, perhaps because of the trade winds that blew across the sea and fanned the air before it reached inland. She sat up, and as she shifted her body to get out of the bed, her hand accidentally swung against the side of her handbag next to her and it fell on the polished wood floor with a thump.

"Everything okay?" Mrs. Lowell called out from the room below. "Do you need help?"

Lila cracked open the bedroom door. "Just my handbag," she called back. "It was on the bed. I forgot it was there."

"You slept well?"

Lila glanced at her watch. *Nine o'clock. I slept almost twelve hours?* "Yes, yes," she said quickly. "Very well, thank you. I'll be down soon."

"Take your time. I'm not much of a cook, but I can make eggs."

"Oh, I don't want to cause you any trouble."

"No trouble at all."

She would be happy to make the eggs, Lila said.

"No trouble," Mrs. Lowell repeated.

So Lila quietly closed the door and hurried to the shower. In less than half an hour she was downstairs fully dressed in slacks and a light sweater.

Mrs. Lowell had made a pot of tea. "I like it too," she said, when Lila thanked her and said tea was the first thing she drank in the morning. "Coffee makes me fidgety."

She had set the table in her tiny kitchen: a pretty blue tablecloth, pink cup and matching saucer, plates with flower patterns, thick white paper napkins.

"I hope you don't mind paper. Years ago, I only used cloth napkins, but now they make paper ones that are just as good."

Her paper napkins were lovely, Lila said. The nicest she had ever seen.

Mrs. Lowell turned the switch under the frying pan on the stove. Lila did her best to stop her but Mrs. Lowell refused; she wanted to make the eggs. "You are my guest," she said.

"It's kind of you, Mrs. Lowell, but I can't have you doing this for me."

The woman's eyes twinkled mischievously. "Just for the first day. Not every day. Sunny side or scrambled?"

Reluctantly, Lila said scrambled, and having no other choice she sat down at the table.

"You had a caller early this morning." Mrs. Lowell

passed a platter of eggs and bacon to Lila. "I think it was just after seven."

"My fiancé? Robert?" Lila was not surprised that he would call. Their last conversation had not ended well. She had accused Robert of unfairly judging the woman who was on the ground, next to the dead man. She had told him that the woman was well-dressed. She looked as though she could have been some kind of professional, a lawyer, a teacher, a doctor, a businesswoman working for a big corporation. Robert laughed. He said she had no idea about what goes on in America. Yes, in middle-class, upper-class America! He was certain the well-dressed woman she described was a heroin addict. Naloxone is a drug that could prevent a drug addict from dying of an overdose, he explained.

Lila had no defense. So Robert added one more reason to the list he kept for why she should return home. "You don't understand Americans, Lila. The drug situation there is not the same as back home. Back home we transport, we sell to the big countries. In America, people buy; they have the money. You can't judge a druggie by the clothes they wear."

"No. Sorry." Mrs. Lowell spooned some more scrambled eggs onto Lila's plate. "Not your fiancé. It was a woman who called. One of the faculty from the college. She seemed anxious to talk to you. Elaine! That was her name. Dr. Elaine McLean. She said she met you."

It could only be the woman who had pleaded with the police not to shoot the man. She had disappeared when the shots rang out. Or perhaps she hadn't, for Lila was already enveloped in a thick black fog. "It must be someone I met yesterday after I got out of the taxi," Lila said softly. "I didn't know her name."

"I hope you don't think it's presumptuous of me, but she said she wanted to take you to lunch, and I told her you'd like that. I thought it would be good for you to meet some of the faculty. Dr. Campbell said she'll be tied up most of the day, but she'll come to see you later."

Dr. Elaine McLean was tall and big-boned. She had full substantial breasts and a pronounced rounded bottom (on Lila's island they would say a *high bottom*), but her hips were slim and her waist fairly narrow. Like most of the women on her island, Lila was petite. She was barely five feet tall, her friends either under that height or above it by a mere inch or two. Aesthetics being as they are, prejudicial, defined by cultural norms of specific regions which have their own standards of beauty, Lila had not considered that a woman who was almost six feet could be beautiful. Beautiful women, in her estimation, were much shorter, but when Dr. McLean rang the doorbell of Mrs. Lowell's home and Lila answered it, she was blown away. Stylish in a modern ethnic way, Dr. McLean exuded the kind of elegance Lila associated with the fashionable women who belonged to her grandmother's bridge club, smart women who outmaneuvered their male opponents, who took as much pride in their outward appearance—hair, clothes, shoes, makeup—as they did in their sharp wit and intellect. Dr. McLean was not dressed as they would have, in a suit or sheath dress. The independence Lila's island had won was political, not necessarily cultural. Fashionable women still took their cues from England;

none would have looked to Africa for style. But Dr. McLean was wearing a decidedly African or West African–inspired outfit: a short-sleeved cotton blouse in geometric patterns of red, green, yellow, and blue kente prints; it hung loosely over a matching ankle-length tight-fitting pencil skirt. The effect was stunning.

Lila had seen her before, of course, but the circumstances were different. Then, shoved to the ground by the police officers, Dr. McLean's face had been contorted with pain and anger. Now, as she stood before Lila, her hand extended in greeting, that face, crumpled the day before, had softened, and she seemed to Lila one of the most beautiful women she had ever met, every feature on her face laid out symmetrically as though composed by the Ultimate Artist, which Lila, though no longer religious, that is churchgoing, could easily imagine the Creator, the Divine, doing, setting eyes evenly spaced on a perfectly oval face, a nose slanting downward to spread out slightly at the ends, a purpled mouth, lips bow-shaped.

"I can't tell you how sorry I am that we had to meet in such a terrible situation. I was coming to Mrs. Lowell to welcome you to Mayfield, and then . . ." Lila glimpsed again in her eyes the despair that had unleashed an outpouring of tears when she screamed, *Don't shoot! Please don't shoot!*

Instinctively, Lila put her arms around Dr. McLean and drew her to her chest. "So kind of you to come," she said, releasing her just as quickly. "Thinking of me after what happened to your friend."

Mrs. Lowell came toward them. "Terrible accident," she said, shaking her head. "I told Lila it's happened before. They need to put a traffic light at that corner. I'm so sorry Lila had to be there. And you too, Dr. McLean."

"Elaine," the visitor said. "Call me Elaine." The expression on her face was inscrutable. Her lips parted as if she were about to smile, but when she spoke again, her voice was weighted with a dark seriousness. "It was no accident, Mrs. Lowell," she said. "My friend was killed in cold blood."

"Killed? Your friend? Surely not . . ." Mrs. Lowell turned to Lila. "Dr. Campbell. She was to call me last night. It must have been late when she got home."

"Didn't you hear the gunshots?" Dr. McLean asked.

Mrs. Lowell was still looking at Lila expectantly. Lila lowered her head.

"You must have heard," Dr. McLean insisted.

"Gunshots?" Mrs. Lowell pressed her fingers to her lips. And once again it seemed to Lila that Mrs. Lowell was forcing herself to control thoughts that were threatening to bubble up on her tongue. "I didn't hear gunshots." She was almost whispering.

Lila felt a wave of pity. She was an old woman who had lived in the town for decades. She would not be able to withstand the shattering of the wholesome image of the town that had comforted her for years. So Lila tried to distract her: "Dr. Campbell will tell you all about it, Mrs. Lowell."

But the old woman was not so easily distracted. "Gunshots? Surely not for a car accident."

Lila held her breath; Dr. McLean was going to contradict Mrs. Lowell. Instead, Dr. McLean held out her hand to Mrs. Lowell, who took it. "It was a pleasure meeting you, Mrs. Lowell, but I have to take Lila away now. I've made reservations."

Mrs. Lowell dropped her hand. "Reservations. Yes, reservations." She brushed away a wisp of hair that had fallen near her eyes.

"Lunch," Dr. McLean said.

Lila quickly grasped the rope Dr. McLean had extended to her. "I'm looking forward to seeing more of the town," she said.

Mrs. Lowell sniffed and a nervous smile creased her lips. "Then I guess you better get going," she said.

Outside, in the street, Lila fished around in her brain to find some excuse for Mrs. Lowell's obvious attempt to deny Dr. McLean's stark accusation that her friend was killed in cold blood. "She's just like my grandmother," Lila said. "My grandmother sees what she wants to see and hears what she wants to hear. She and Mrs. Lowell want the world to remain the same as they remember it."

"She heard the sirens," Dr. McLean said flatly.

"She said it was a car accident. She thought a student was hurt."

"And you believe her?"

Lila did not respond.

"Dr. Ron Brown was my friend, a professor."

"He teaches at Mayfield?"

"*Taught.* Taught at Mayfield. He is dead. Killed in cold blood."

The words stark, said without elaboration, choked Lila into silence. She was there. She had seen the police officer with his gun drawn, his finger on the trigger. She had heard Dr. McLean call out her friend's name, beg for his life. Then the shots. He fell, and she saw the rivulet of blood streaming down his cheek.

"They took him away," Dr. McLean said bitterly. "There'll be an inquest, but we know what happened."

They were walking toward Main Street. Lila swallowed the knot in her throat and asked the question she hoped would not give her the answer she feared. "Is the restaurant we're going to near where it happened?"

"Where Ron was killed? No, we're not going to pass there. The restaurant is on a side street. We won't be passing the barrels of flowers." She grimaced. "Pretty Main Street," she scoffed. "No, we won't be going down pretty Main Street."

Lila had admired the flowers that dotted the sidewalks on Main Street. Now all she could see in her mind's eye was blood.

"You were brave," Dr. McLean said.

"Brave?"

"You stayed."

"How did you know . . . ?"

"That it was you who helped me?" Dr. McLean laughed. "Have you seen anyone looking like you since you arrived?"

"You mean . . . ?"

"Yes."

Lila rubbed her forehead. "I fell down," she said. "They pushed me down, the people who were running away."

"But you didn't go away."

"A man helped me up."

"But you stayed," Dr. McLean repeated.

"I had no choice."

"You could have been killed too. I couldn't take that chance. They had killed Ron. I could have been next. *You!*"

"Me?"

"Yes, you too. I ran as fast as I could," Dr. McLean said. "You should have too." She faced Lila. "But you saw, didn't you?"

"I was there."

"But didn't you see when they shot Ron?"

Something was holding Lila back from responding. Was it Robert saying to her: *Don't get mixed up in this, Lila?* "I was still on the sidewalk." This was as far as she would commit herself.

"Well, I'm glad you were there," Dr. McLean said. "I'm glad you saw."

But Lila had not said that; she had not said she saw.

There were two people seated at the restaurant waiting to have lunch with her, a man and a woman. They were the only other Black people she had seen in Mayfield.

"And we are the only Black people you *will* see in this town," Dr. McLean said, responding to Lila's remark as they approached the table. "Four of us in all. Or were. Now one of us is dead."

Lila was thankful that she had not added, *Killed in cold blood.*

The man's name was Terrence Carter. He was tall, lanky, and sinewy. Long dreadlocks grazed the collar of his shirt-jack, a style that had become popular on her island in the years after Independence when, sensibly, men threw off the wool suit jackets they were made to wear in colonial times for something lighter, though still formal. It surprised her that here too, in America, men also wore shirt-jacks. *Perhaps only Black men.*

The bones on the man's face were like scaffolding holding up his cheeks. They hollowed out his eyes and carved out a brow that gave him a look of intensity, seriousness, intelligence. His brown skin lacked luster and paled against the rich chocolate-brown complexion of the woman who was sitting next to him. Her name was Gail Cooper. She was slightly overweight and short. She wore a loose print blouse and black knit skirt that fell unattractively to her ankles. Her shoes were orthopedics, black, laced. She remained sitting when Dr. McLean introduced her.

"Gail works in the bursar's office," Dr. McLean said. "She's a genius with figures. Should be the bursar, but in this place . . ."

"Let's not start that," Gail said, frowning. "I do my job, I get paid, I feed my family." She shook her head and the flesh beneath her chin jiggled. "Welcome to Mayfield," she greeted Lila.

Terrence was already standing. "We've been waiting a long time for you," he said.

"Perhaps Dr. McLean and I should have walked faster, Dr. Carter," Lila said apologetically.

"First names, please. We are colleagues."

"Terrence," Lila said. "I probably was at fault, not Elaine. I walk slowly."

Terrence grinned. "I meant we've been waiting for someone *like you*." He towered over her, but when he spoke he bent down slightly to ease the distance between them.

"Like *me*?"

"You couldn't ever walk that fast," he said, smiling grimly. He shook her hand. It was a warm handshake. He was sinewy, but his grasp was firm. "I meant years. We've been waiting years for you."

Gail intervened: "Sorry you had to come at such a bad time, Lila."

"It's not your fault," Lila said, still puzzled by Terrence's comment. It had been less than a year since she accepted the offer from Mayfield.

"This isn't the best place in the world," Gail said, "but we've never had an incident . . ."

"It wasn't an incident," Elaine said quietly, but there was no mistaking her objection to the word Gail had used.

Gail turned to Lila. "Nothing like that has ever happened before." She glanced at Elaine, who lowered her head and did not respond. "It was an aberration."

"I know he was your colleague," Lila said. "That had to be hard for you."

Elaine looked up. "He didn't have a chance."

Gail touched Elaine's hand lightly.

"I tried to stop them, but they were aiming their guns at him," Elaine said.

"There'll be an inquest," Gail said.

"It'll take a week."

"An inquest will be good," Gail said.

"A week is too long."

"And a trial," Gail said. "We want a trial, don't we?"

"Convicting a white police officer for killing a Black man?" Terrence scoffed. His long legs twitched.

"Maybe this time," Gail said.

A dark shadow crossed over their faces. Lila wished

she could find the words to let them know how sorry she was for their loss. She was an outsider. She could sympathize, but she could not feel their pain. Not really.

"Like a dog," Terrence was saying. "Just shot him like a stray dog."

"They didn't care. Ron was a nobody to them," Elaine said, then patted Terrence's arm.

"Black men are an endangered species," Terrence said.

Gail began weeping silently. A waiter approached. He stopped briefly, looked over at them, and walked on.

They were talking to each other now as if she were not there. Words passed back and forth from one to the other. Lila could barely distinguish them.

Eventually, Elaine broke away. "We're making Lila uncomfortable," she said.

"No, no," Lila said quickly. "I understand. I imagine you have a lot to talk about. To do."

"There's nothing we can do now anyway until the inquest," Terrence said.

"So let's sit. Sit." Elaine gestured to the chairs.

Terrence stood aside until she and Lila were seated.

"We wanted you to meet us," Elaine said. "We made this reservation last week. We wanted to meet you before you met the others. Ron . . . It was his idea."

"It's okay," Lila said. "We don't have to stay. We can have lunch another day."

"No. We are here now. We want you to know you have friends at Mayfield, people you can count on. Ron would have wanted us to meet before the others get to you."

Get to me? Lila's eyebrows shot up.

Gail quickly clarified: "The faculty are nice, well meaning. I think what Elaine is trying to say is that we can prepare you for them. Ron thought . . . Ron said that . . ." She paused again and glanced at Terrence.

Terrence took over: "I think it's the first time you'll be teaching at an American college. Is that right, Lila? It must be different from your university in the Caribbean, right?"

"So it was Ron's idea that we fill you in," Gail said. "The nuances . . ."

Furrows gathered between Lila's eyebrows. She turned to Terrence, waiting for him to explain.

"I expect you were in the majority on your island," he said. "Here, we are in the minority. In this country, in this college. There are differences."

"I thought that was all over," Lila said. "The Civil Rights Movement . . ."

"Ended legal segregation, yes. But you can't legislate people's hearts, what they feel, how they think."

Lila felt foolish. Was her response wishful thinking? She knew the stories of racial injustice and violence in America. She didn't have to be told that laws do not change hearts. Perhaps she simply wanted to believe what Gail had said: what had happened yesterday in Mayfield was an aberration. She was safe here.

Elaine reached for the glass in front of her and swallowed down the water in quick gulps. "Ron," she said.

One word and silence thickened between them.

Finally, Gail spoke up: "Tell us about *you*, Lila. How did you find your way here to this small college, in this small town?"

"Her essay," Terrence said.

"You know about my essay?" Lila said, relieved that the conversation had turned away from Ron.

"I gave it to Dr. Campbell."

"So I owe my appointment to you?"

"I can't take credit for that. Dr. Campbell had other problems and you were just the person she needed."

"We all read your essay," Elaine said. "Terrence was not joking when he said that we have been waiting a long time in this college for someone like you. Years."

The waiter came again. This time he seemed determined to collect their orders.

Elaine took charge: "Collard greens, candied yams." She tapped the menu card. "And the chicken."

"Grilled, not fried," Terrence said.

Elaine grinned. "This is the only restaurant in this town that serves Black food," she said, turning to Lila, "and Terrence here . . ."

"They don't have the 'real Black food,'" Gail intervened.

"They make a good fried chicken," Elaine responded. "But Terrence won't eat it."

Terrence groaned. "Fried chicken is killing our people. The oil clogs up the arteries in the heart."

"Ron was always teasing Terrence about his weight," Elaine said. "He told him he'd have more fat on his bones if he ate more fried chicken. Look at him, all skin and bones!"

Terrence thumped his chest. "And abs."

Elaine laughed. It was not a full-throated laugh, but Lila was glad to hear it. Elaine had talked about Ron and she had not mentioned his death.

"So you think you'd like collard greens?" Terrence asked Lila.

"She probably doesn't know what it is," Elaine said.

"I'm willing to try it," Lila said.

"You'll love it," Gail said. "And the biscuits too. It's not the same as the biscuits down south, but it's a good imitation."

She liked the collard greens. They reminded her of the callaloo that people on her island made from dasheen bush. The biscuits were surprising, pleasantly so. They were flaky and the layers separated easily like thin plates.

"When you said biscuits," Lila said, "I thought you meant the kind we buy in tins."

"We call those crackers," Terrence said.

"Crackers! That's who they were," Elaine said, and for some reason that Lila could not understand, the word seemed to make her sad again.

6

D r. Campbell had already arrived at Mrs. Lowell's home when Lila came back from lunch. She got up quickly from the armchair where she was sitting opposite to Mrs. Lowell, and practically ran toward Lila. "Oh my dear, oh my dear, I am so sorry I wasn't here to greet you." She wrapped her arms around Lila. "So, so sorry." She released Lila from her embrace, but holding her hand, she turned to Mrs. Lowell. "You didn't tell me she was beautiful."

Lila shook her head. "You're so kind, Dr. Campbell. I don't think—"

"But you are! Look at those eyes!" She stepped back and, keeping Lila at arm's length, gushed some more: "What a beautiful complexion! The sun must have done this to you. We don't have much sun here. Just a few months, and even that . . ."

Lila searched for words to return the compliment. Dr. Campbell's skin was dry and floury, without even the slightest hint of makeup, no color above her eyes, no color on her cheeks, none on her lips. Though she appeared to be in her forties, her hair was completely gray. It was cut in a short style as if by a barber rather than a hairdresser. She had on tan slacks, a buttoned-up blue shirt, and a shapeless navy blazer. Her only concession to the severity of her looks were her shoes; they were spiked heels, three inches high. She had greeted Lila warmly, but her physical appearance gave the impression that she was a single-minded academic who had no time for personal interactions.

"Where I come from we have sun all year round," Lila conceded. "I expect I will look different in the winter months."

"Well, welcome to Mayfield. We have been looking forward to your arrival. I hope we didn't frighten you yesterday." Dr. Campbell turned to Mrs. Lowell again. "So tiny."

"And strong," Mrs. Lowell said. "She walked all the way from Main Street with her luggage."

"I had help," Lila said, and explained more fully how she arrived at Mrs. Lowell's.

"It was a terrible situation," Dr. Campbell said.

"Dr. McLean, Dr. Carter, and Ms. Cooper took me to lunch. They told me about Dr. Brown."

Dr. Campbell pursed her lips and the muscles on the sides of her face grew rigid. "He was in the wrong place at the wrong time," she said.

Lila thought it best not to respond.

For a second, in that silence when Lila did not react, Dr. Campbell frowned, but then seeming to think it better to put Lila at ease rather than frighten her, she said, smiling now, "Mayfield is a wonderful town. I want you to know that, Lila. You'll like it here. The college is great. Good students, friendly faculty. You'll be safe at Mayfield."

"I told her so," Mrs. Lowell said.

"I don't know why Dr. Brown was in front of that restaurant in the middle of the day. Perhaps we will never know. That poor woman." Dr. Campbell shook her downturned head.

"What the family must be going through now," Mrs. Lowell said.

"They took her to the hospital," Dr. Campbell said. "She'll recover."

It was on the tip of Lila's tongue to say that Ron Brown would never recover, but now it struck her that no one at lunch had mentioned the woman. It was as if she were not there, though as far as Lila could tell, she was the reason the police had trained their guns on Ron Brown.

Dr. Campbell faced Lila again. "I want to assure you that everything will be all right. Things are quiet on campus. What happened won't affect you at all." She glanced at Mrs. Lowell and their eyes met. "Political Science," she said. "That was his department. They take sides there—liberal, conservative, left, right. Very contentious. I'll say this for Ron Brown: no one argued a position better than he did." She worked her lips over her teeth. "He wouldn't have fit in my department, though. We take the middle road."

"Gadfly," Mrs. Lowell murmured.

Dr. Campbell grimaced and Mrs. Lowell, apparently intuiting the expression on Dr. Campbell's face as a signal to her to say no more, clasped her hand over her mouth and shook her head.

"Now he's dead," Lila said quietly.

Dr. Campbell shot her a hard glance but just as quickly her eyes softened. "Yes," she said. "And that is unfortunate. We'll get more details after the inquest, but Ron should have known better."

* * *

Alone in her room, Lila called Robert, Dr. Campbell's words ringing in her ears. What should Ron have known better? Should he have been killed because he hesitated for a moment to put up his hands? For Lila believed that in that moment, Ron felt he had no choice. He thought the woman was dying. Why else would he have taken the chance to disobey the police? He must have known they had guns.

When Lila finally told Robert that the man who died was a professor at the college, his reaction was what she had expected: "I didn't want you to go, but at least I thought you'd be safe at a university."

Lila tried to convince him that Mayfield was a quiet town, that nothing like that had ever happened before.

Robert was sympathetic; after all, a man had died. But he couldn't blame the police, he said. They had warned Ron to move away from the woman and Ron had ignored the order.

"Perhaps he didn't hear them," Lila said, making a desperate attempt to shut out the word she had heard so clearly, though Mrs. Lowell had lowered her voice almost to a whisper. Gadfly, she had called Ron. *They had talked about the killing; they had taken sides*. How the irony had escaped them both! Dr. Campbell did not want Dr. Brown in her department. He was a man who took sides, she said.

And what side, whose side, had Ron taken as he straddled the woman, as he brought his lips down on her mouth? Surely he wasn't a fool. He wouldn't have gambled with his life.

"He wasn't deaf," Robert was saying. "You can't believe that, Lila. He could hear."

"Maybe. But I think he was trying to help the woman. Didn't you tell me she was an addict? He was blowing air into her mouth. Maybe she couldn't breathe."

"But she didn't die. Maybe she could breathe all right on her own."

"After they gave her the naloxone," Lila said flatly, not masking her sarcasm. "Until then, Dr. Brown kept her alive."

Robert groaned. "You are not listening to me, Lila. When a police officer orders you to do something, you obey him. How was the police to know Ron wasn't trying to hurt the woman or, God forbid, kill her."

"Elaine told the police she knew him. She told them that Ron taught at the college."

"I really don't think that's enough, Lila. When you are in a life-and-death situation, you just can't take the word of some random woman."

"Why do you say she was a random woman? She was Dr. Brown's colleague."

"Hmm."

"Is it because she's a Black woman?"

Robert sighed deeply. "Lila, Lila, I warned you. You don't understand."

"And what is it I don't understand, Robert?"

"I warned you not to get involved in America's racial problem."

And when had he warned her? Was it when she read her essay to him? Literature was not his forte; he was a tradesman; buying and selling was his business, how he made a living.

He intended to read the essay, he had said to her, as soon as things settled down with the contract he was working on, but he kept putting it off. Then Lila told him about the offer from Mayfield and his curiosity was piqued. This was something he understood: getting profitable returns for one's investment. Quid pro quo.

He had listened silently while she read the essay to him. It was about Shakespeare's *The Tempest*, or, rather, about the response of Caribbean writers to the West's interpretation of the play, particularly their analysis of Prospero and Caliban. In the essay, Lila defended Caribbean writers who took issue with Western critics for praising Prospero as a representative of Art, of all things Good, and yet were untroubled by Prospero's denigration of Caliban as an unredeemable savage from a tropical island (*an island too much like my own homeland*, Lila had written), a creature whose "vile race" was such that "good natures" could not abide with.

Robert made no comment about her argument, though from time to time he frowned and cleared his throat.

"What makes me angry," Lila had said, "is that while they have no problem castigating Caliban, they are happy to appropriate his island and to appropriate his beautiful words."

Robert laughed. "Appropriate? Why would the West want to appropriate Caliban's island or even his words?"

Lila read the parts of her essay where she had taken a not-so-subtle swipe at the West's apparent change of heart at the opening ceremony of the 2012 Olympic Games. There, in London, on the top of a hill, were Englishmen in black frock coats and top hats, greeting the world with Caliban's lyrical words: "Be not afeared. The isle is full of noises, / Sounds, and sweet airs that give delight but hurt not." Surely, the English did not think that Shakespeare meant the isle of Britain, Lila had written. Surely, Caliban, "the savage," was not speaking of England as his home country where a thousand instruments hummed around his ears. Surely, it was not Prospero, the poet, who had delivered those lines, the most beautiful in the play! Page after page, her indignation lighting fire to her words, Lila had written about the hypocrisy on display on that hill outside London, about the irony. *About appropriation.*

Then her essay veered to America, to the disappearance from bookshelves of novels written by Black writers that told the real stories of the Black experience. She named *Native Son*, *Invisible Man*, *Go Tell It on the Mountain*. She argued that novels like these stirred too many bad memories. Now what sold were stories about the Black experience written by white writers. *The Maid* was selling like hotcakes!

Written by a white woman who was raised in the segregated South by her Black nanny, *The Maid* told the story of the Black nanny's experience. Yet who would know better how it feels to leave your young children at home to go to a white woman's home to raise *her* white young children? Lila posed the question in her essay. Would that novel have been as successful if it were written by a Black woman?

"Another case of appropriation!" she said to Robert.

Robert had told her he admired her essay. Caribbean writers would appreciate what she had written, but that part about America was unnecessary. She should delete it. What did she know about America? She didn't live there, she had no relatives who lived there. And yet it was that part about America that had led Terrence to give her essay to Dr. Campbell, who had her own reasons for seizing upon Lila's bold assertions about appropriation to persuade the college president that they needed Lila at Mayfield.

"You are not from America," Robert said now. "America is not your country. Not your business. And there you go accusing me of American prejudice because I said you can't take the word of some random woman."

"She wasn't a random woman. I told you that."

"Okay. Some random *Black* woman then.'"

"Are you trying to annoy me, Robert?"

"I'm trying to get you focused on what you were hired to do. The college hired you to teach. Focus on that."

Her face burned, her head throbbed. "I am Black," Lila snapped.

For long seconds Robert did not speak. Lila could hear only his breath. He was trying to compose himself, she knew. He was measuring what next he would say to her. And it surprised her too that she had used that word, *Black.* It came out of her mouth before she could stop it, and she couldn't stop it because it was an utterance from her heart, from her very soul, from deep inside of her. She was a Bonnard, but her mother was not a Bonnard by blood. African blood dominated any other blood that might have flowed through her mother's veins. Her mother's skin was dark, the deep brown of a tamarind shell. She had dark eyes, full lips, and a nose that fit perfectly on her oval face and was broad, flattened at the bridge below her eyes. Yes, if she was anything, Lila thought, she was Black. When she uttered the word, it had no political significance to her. It was a statement of her identity, her connection to her past. Her connection to the woman Robert ridiculed.

Robert took a deep breath before he spoke again. "If anything," he said, his voice strong, "you are colored."

"No one says colored anymore, Robert."

"Well, you are not Black. You just can't deny all your other bloods, all your other family," he said.

"In America, you have to choose."

"There you go again, Lila. America has a problem; we don't."

"You say we don't because you have the advantage that comes with being light-skinned on our island. We may not have Black and white racism as they have in America, but we have colorism."

"Colorism?" he sneered. "Is that a new word you invented?"

"You know exactly what I mean. The lighter the skin, the more jobs you get, the more money you have."

She had not invented the word. She had read it in the writings of the Jamaican novelist Michelle Cliff. In Jamaica, Michelle Cliff was considered white (though in America they would count the number of drops of Black blood that ran in her veins). Nevertheless, she knew firsthand the privilege her pale skin had given her in Jamaica. It was her family's passport to wealth, she wrote. Malcolm Gladwell, the highly successful writer, had not used the word in his wildly popular book *Outliers*, but he admitted that his Black family had gained the "privilege of color" in Jamaica when the son of his Irish great-great-great-grandfather had a child with an Igbo woman from West Africa.

"You never talked this way, Lila," Robert grumbled.

"I never saw a man shot dead just because his skin is black," she said.

7

Why had she accepted Robert's marriage proposal? Her friends claimed Robert caught her on the rebound. Her affair with him was not based on true love but on desperation, they said. She had been hurt by Kenton, the man she had loved for years, and was simply trying to replace him.

Lila had met Kenton in her last year at graduate school. She had fallen in love with him almost immediately. It was his eyes that captivated her heart. They were big and brown and deep. It was as if he could see more than the world around them, as if his mind traveled great distances across the ocean into lands that seemed as familiar to him as his own. Africa, he said, was the source of all life, the beginning of the beginning when man first walked on the earth. He talked to her of the Zulus who fought the British with their spears and shields though they faced certain death when bullets rained down on them. Nelson Mandela was his hero. Twenty-seven years in prison, most of the time spent in solitary confinement or breaking stones in Robben Island. But nothing broke Mandela, Kenton said.

He was completing a PhD in political science when Lila met him. She was an English literature major. At times Kenton would accuse her of being elitist, saying she seemed more interested in a fictive world than in the real world where every day there were new atrocities and people were suffering, in dire need of food and shelter. She would argue that stories bring these worlds to life and touch the hearts of people. People empathize with the characters' pain, she said. She even quoted Aristotle. She talked about pity and fear. The catharsis. "And what difference does catharsis make?" Kenton had asked. "Catharsis may make you feel better; you have taken a load off your shoulders, but does catharsis make the world better? It doesn't matter what people *feel*; it matters what they *do*." Eventually, though, Kenton would relent before she could, and he would fold her in his arms. She loved him for that—that he would not allow their differences to blow up into irreparable quarrels—but she was always aware of his eyes drifting beyond her, even when he held her to his heart.

It didn't surprise her when he announced that after he graduated, he was going to Africa, to Niger. He wanted to do his part, he said. To help the children there.

Lila could not locate Niger in Africa; she thought it was part of Nigeria. He corrected her gently but she could tell by the way his eyes narrowed that her mistake had probably cemented his decision to go without her. Still she begged. She said she could not part from him. She loved him. He said he loved her too.

"Then why?"

"Look at us," he said, and stretched out his bare arm and laid it against hers. The starkness of their difference was something she could not contest. Her skin was the color of coffee drenched in milk. His was the color of pitch, black, shiny. "You have loyalties, Lila, that I do not have. You are a Bonnard; I am a Cudjoe."

Cudjoe: the name of the African, the Maroon leader who outwitted the British and hid runaway slaves in the Blue Mountains of Jamaica. Bonnard: the progeny of French planters, slave owners in the Caribbean.

How his family came to own the name, Kenton could not tell her; he had no facts to verify his claim. All he knew was that for generations his family were Cudjoes. His skin was his evidence.

Kenton never said that Lila's café au lait skin was the impenetrable barrier between them. He said he could not subject her to the harsh life that he intended to pursue. He said he did not plan to live in the city, in Niamey. He was going to teach in the villages, in the remote places where children had not been taught to read and write. Where there was no running water. Where they had outhouses, not fancy toilets.

When he left, Lila was devastated. She cried for weeks. Then a friend introduced her to Robert.

Lila could not say that she was immediately attracted to Robert. She did not feel that rush of excitement that burned her cheeks the first time she met Kenton and he touched her hand. Robert put her at ease; she was comfortable with him, relaxed. He was familiar, like someone she had known all her life. Like her family.

Her grandmother liked him right away, Lila suspected because she was relieved that her romance with Kenton had ended. Kenton was too African, she said. Lila knew she meant he was too black. When she protested that Kenton was born and raised on the same island as both of them, her grandmother had responded, "He's not like us."

Us. The Bonnards were Roman Catholics, and not

just Catholics but Poto L'Église, the Pillars of the Catholic Church. The sons of Bonnards were altar boys, daughters nuns, uncles priests. The Easter and Corpus Christi processions began not far from the Bonnard family home, next to the Bonnard family church and the Bonnard family cemetery, and wound itself through the streets, up and down the hills of their prosperous village, and back to the family home where the Bonnards spread out a banquet of tea and cakes and sweets on the veranda, a bottle or two covered discreetly for the priests and decanted in pastel-colored water glasses so no one knew they had imbibed until they were seen stumbling back to the rectory.

Kenton was not a Catholic; he was a Baptist but not a churchgoing adherent, yet he fiercely defended the sect that called themselves Baptist Shouters. "They are the Baptists who have not forgotten their African past," he said.

Unlike the Catholics, who were generally reserved, the Baptist Shouters made a public display of their religious fervor. They frequently held their ceremonies in the front of rum shops and called their followers to their service with a brass bell they rang incessantly. They shook their tambourines and beat their drums as they hailed fire and brimstone on sinners. They dressed in white, the men in shirts and pants, the women in long dresses and headwraps tied in elaborate bows in front of their heads. Kenton admired them, but they were often the laughingstock of the island's elite. Of people like the Bonnards.

Robert was not a descendant of the Poto L'Église, but he was a Catholic, so he was acceptable to Lila's grandmother, and not in a small way because he too was mixed. He had ancestors who were African but more who were European. He was what on Lila's island would be called high brown or red, his color that of a white man who was permanently tanned. He had curly dark-brown hair and light eyes and his lips, though not thin, were not as full as the darker-skinned men. All would have gone well when Lila announced her intention to marry Robert had Lila's grandmother not discovered that Robert was divorced.

Of the Bonnards, Lila's grandmother, Agnes, was the holiest, the one who adhered most rigidly to all Catholic dogmas. She believed one married for life; the holy bond of marriage can be severed only by death. She believed in heaven, she believed in the burning fires of hell, she believed her beloved granddaughter would be condemned to eternal damnation if she married a divorcé, so she pleaded with Lila to give up Robert. But Lila had spent her twenties in love with a man she expected to marry and it had taken her a long time to recover and trust a man again. Robert gave her the confidence she needed, the assurance that he would never leave her. They had been dating for just six months when he asked her to marry him. To her friends, that was not enough time to make a commitment for life. For Lila, proof of love was someone's willingness to make such a commitment. She had believed Kenton loved her and yet he left her. She would not make the mistake again of confusing true love with romance. If Kenton truly loved her, he would have taken her with him; he would have married her.

And yet she had not fought back when Kenton spoke of their loyalties. Was she more loyal to the Bonnards and to what they represented? She buried the question; she would not allow herself to think too deeply on what the answer might reveal about herself.

Robert was a businessman. He was a practical man. He had no time for "navel gazing," he said. He knew what he liked and he went after what he wanted. And he liked Lila; he loved her; he wanted to spend the rest of his life with her.

His certainty, his resolve, his lack of any doubt or hesitation, was thrilling for Lila. Her head spun with his promises, his pledge to her that he would never abandon her. He was not like Kenton. Not like her parents.

An absurd comparison. Unfair. Yet her need was deep and reason had not healed her. A car accident had taken her parents away from her, and the hole they left in her heart had never been filled.

"Think of your immortal soul," her grandmother begged her. "Think of the next world."

The arrival of Dr. Mary Campbell's invitation had been fortuitous. Lila did not share her grandmother's religious convictions; she did not believe she would be condemned to eternal fires if she married Robert, but she was also aware that her feelings for Robert were quite different from the passion she'd felt for Kenton.

If she accepted Mary Campbell's invitation she would have more time to consider Robert's proposal free from the pressure of his constant, and, she acceded, sensible, persuasive arguments. It would strengthen her confidence in her decision that in choosing Robert, she was choosing her happiness. Her grandmother would continue to fear for her soul, but her grandmother loved her and in time would forgive her. Ultimately, though, it was Mary Campbell's rapturous overtures in a follow-up e-mail that sealed Lila's conviction that some months' separation would be good for both her and Robert and would prove that their relationship could last a lifetime.

8

Lila was on her way to her office on the first day of class when she heard a male voice behind her call out, "Hi!" She turned around and knew immediately who he was. She could not forget those blue eyes.

"I didn't know your name," he said. "And I hadn't given you mine." He stuck out his hand. "Clive. Clive Lewis."

"The Good Samaritan," she said, taking his hand. "Lila. Lila Bonnard."

He grinned. "I don't know about that." He ran his hand through his hair. "You are a beautiful woman."

Involuntarily, Lila lowered her eyes. "So you took advantage of a damsel in distress," she said, smiling, though his remark had made her slightly uncomfortable.

He blushed. "Oh, I don't mean I didn't want to help," he said quickly.

"Thank you," she responded simply.

The redness that stained his cheeks cooled. "You must have been very frightened. You were collapsed on the ground."

"I don't know what I'd have done if you hadn't come along."

"I saw when the students pushed past you."

"So many," she said.

"They were terrified too."

"All that blood. That poor man. Dead."

"Yes." Clive's eyes dimmed.

"Did you know him?"

"In passing. I know the woman, though."

"Mrs. Lowell . . . where I am staying. You dropped me off there. She said the woman comes from a good family."

"Yes."

Lila was curious, but the finality in his tone told her not to press him.

"So where are you from, Lila Bonnard?" he asked.

"An island in the Caribbean."

"No name?"

"You wouldn't know it. St. Marie. It's an offshore island close to Grenada."

"Grenada? I know Grenada. I've heard of Grenada."

"The American invasion. My island was geographically close but politically very far away."

He did not ask her to explain further and she was pleasantly surprised. He simply said, "Was your island safe from us?"

Lila shrugged. "We had nothing anyone wanted."

He laughed. "Except sea and sun."

"The tourists haven't found us yet." She looked down at her briefcase. "I'm sorry, I have to get going. My class starts in half an hour."

"You're teaching at the college." It was more of a statement than a question.

"I am . . . or I will be," she said. "But I have to get to my office first. To prepare."

"I won't hold you up, but can we meet after your class for coffee? There's a café nearby."

"Will they have tea?" she asked.

He clapped his hands. "Tea it will be."

"I'll be in my office. Say, two hours from now?"

She gave him the number of her office and as he was writing it down, he said, "I meant it. You are beautiful."

On the pathway toward her office, Lila could feel her heart racing. She told herself it was because she was walking fast; she did not want to be late. But she had more than half an hour before her class would begin and she had to admit there was no other explanation for her rapid heartbeat and the tingling at the tips of her fingers except for her sudden nervousness when she looked away and Clive persisted. "It's true," he had said.

She allowed that her dark eyes, black curly hair, and café au lait complexion would have been interesting to a man like Clive, a white man living in Vermont. He would find her exotic. Robert admired her skin tone too. He compared the color of her skin to liquid caramel that he said flowed without a blotch from her head to her feet. She had the body of a teenager, he said. Her friends said the same, complimenting her for her tiny waist, slim hips, flat belly. They already had children, some more than two, and their hips and waists had spread, their stomachs, it seemed, permanently rounded. They envied her and yet she would have traded her flat stomach for a child with Kenton.

Lila sighed. The past was the past. Gone. Robert was her fiancé, and she accepted his praise in that context. He loved her; he wanted to please her. She sighed again but this time a smile curled around the edges of her lips. Clive Lewis did not know her; he did not have to please her.

From the way he was dressed—hooded sweatshirt, blue jeans, white sneakers—she concluded that Clive was probably a student. But she had detected white strands among his light-brown hair and she noticed that the lines around his nose and mouth had already begun to deepen, so it was likely he was closer to her age than the average college student. Then suddenly it occurred to her that he might think *she* was much older than he was. *And if he does, what does it matter?* she said to herself, irritated that such a thought would have crossed her mind.

She had put on a navy pants suit that morning and buttoned up the jacket to the collar, letting only the tip of her white shirt soften the severity of her outfit. Navy, she was told, was the color that telegraphed power, pants projected competence. Still, she found herself wishing she had worn a dress, one that flattered her figure. She unbuttoned the top of her jacket and flattened the collar of her white shirt over it. She exhaled and smiled. The slight change made her look less stiff and formal.

Dr. Campbell had given her a corner office on the fourth floor of the main academic building. Most of the classrooms were on the first and second floors; junior faculty shared the third floor with the remaining classrooms. Senior faculty had their offices on the fourth floor. Lila's office belonged to Dr. Klein, the college's only distinguished professor, a Classics scholar who was on sabbatical.

The two windows in the office were large. Through one of them rolling mountains, peaks and valleys, were visible in the distance, and in the valleys there were clusters of houses. Lila's thoughts leapt to the mountain range that stretched across the north of her island, from the west coast to the east. She lived on the eastern side of the mountains where the land sloped down to the Atlantic. In the mornings she woke up to the call and response of whistling birds and the screeching of skirmishes between the larger feathered ones. She would fill her lungs with the clean scent of rain that fell like a diaphanous curtain from the mountaintop and dissipated as quickly with the morning sun. Here, though, the mountains were higher; they seemed more solid, more formidable, though they were still covered in their summer green.

She could see the lake from the other window. Mrs. Lowell had told her about it. In the summertime, she said, boats with colorful sails skimmed across it, families had picnics on the beach, and, of course, they swam in the water. If Lila walked down to the end of Main Street, she said, she would find it. Lila could not see the lake from her bedroom window, but from her office she had a clear view of the sandy beach. There were no sea-almond trees, no coconut trees, just a blanket of brown sand and water placid, still, the morning sunlight spread out eerily on its surface like a watchful eye warning of vigilance. *Vigilance for what?* Lila shook her head to throw off the sudden chill that snaked up her spine. A professor had been shot dead by the police. Would the good students she was about to teach ask her about Ron Brown? If they did, what would she say?

Lila turned away from the window. Dr. Klein's desk was on the opposite side of the room. It was an enormous desk, an antique fitting for a professor of Ancient Literature. It was made of oak and stood on large lion-paw legs. Around the sides were carvings of vines with long twisting tendrils and odd-shaped leaves. Lila had seen a photograph of Dr. Klein. He was a man of imposing stature with a large head, wild gray Einstein hair, thick ruffled eyebrows, and piercing eyes. His desk faced the door and was flanked by overstuffed bookshelves. Lila wondered if the arrangement of his furniture was deliberate, if he had chosen to sit with the mountains looming behind him to solidify his eminence as a distinguished scholar and professor. She would have the desk moved to the other side of the room where the second window opened up to the lake. Her chair would not be directly in front of the door, but at an angle where students could see her when they entered the room and still have the view of the water. She would only have to turn around, close her eyes, and memories of her Caribbean Sea would come flooding back.

She had taken courses in the Classics at university, so the titles on Dr. Klein's bookshelves that lined two walls of the office were familiar to her. She ran her fingers past the ancient Greeks: Homer, Hesiod, Archilochus, Pindar, Sappho, Aeschylus, Sophocles, Euripides. She pulled out *The Iliad*, the story of the final years of the Trojan War, the last battle between Achilles and Hector. When she learned that her temporary office belonged to a scholar of the Classics, she had put in her briefcase *Omeros*, Derek Walcott's epic poem that catapulted him to the world stage when he won the Nobel Prize. She would begin the class with *Omeros*, with Walcott, the Homeric poet, the Omeros, singing of the triumphs and sorrows of the fishermen from his homeland in St. Lucia. With *Omeros*, she would make the point about our common humanity, our common flaws, hopes, desires, fears. So with *Omeros* and Homer's *Iliad* in her briefcase, she entered the classroom.

The students greeted her with broad smiles. One young woman brought her hands together at her chin and clapped soundlessly. If Ron Brown was on the students' minds, they gave no indication of it. *Things are quiet on the campus*, Dr. Campbell had said. And all was cheerful in her classroom. Lila exhaled; her anxiety subsided. She would teach the lesson she had planned. She wrote her name on the blackboard, *Dr. Lila Bonnard*, and under her name she added her rank, *Associate Professor of English*.

The students gave their names and brief statements about their interest in taking the course. Their parents or relatives had taken a cruise to the Caribbean, they explained. Some had spent long holidays there. At the Hilton, the Ramada, Sandals; they listed tourist hotels by the beach. And they liked reggae music. Bob Marley. They knew all his songs, could recite the lyrics by heart. *He was Jamaican, wasn't he?* They wanted to go to Jamaica one day. To see Tivoli Gardens. *That's where he lived, wasn't it? And the people there are poor, aren't they?*

A student sitting in the third row was scrolling through his iPhone while the others were eagerly asking their questions. He was clearly disengaged from the class. Then, abruptly, he looked up from his iPhone and raised his hand. "I believe Bob Marley was a drug addict," he announced.

"He smoked marijuana," another student countered. "He was not an addict."

"It says here." The young man tapped his iPhone. "It says here that Jamaica has one of the highest murder rates in the world. The crime rate per capita is higher than in the US. It says that it's because of the drugs in Jamaica."

It was not the story Lila wanted to tell. Not right now. Not on the first day of class, but she could not deny it. In 2005, Jamaica had the highest murder rate in the world, the numbers barely declining in recent times. Without natural resources, the island depends heavily on tourism, which provides for some but leaves most in desperate poverty. Gangs have surfaced, kidnappings; there is violence in the streets, politicians accused of corruption, all fighting for a share in the profitable drug trade. But that is not the whole story of Jamaica; it does not tell of the beauty of the place, the thick emerald-green foliage, the brilliant colors of flowers that grow wild, the undulating hills and mountains crowned by dazzling blue skies and cotton-white clouds, the glistening rivers and magnificent waterfalls, the turquoise sea, white sands. It does not tell of the artists whose works rival the best in the world, the university that has produced some of the finest professionals and thinkers. The writers who vie successfully for the world's top literary prizes.

The young man with the iPhone raised his hand again, but before he could speak another student jumped in, a young woman, pretty, dark-haired, flashing eyes. "Well, I like Nicki Minaj and Rihanna," she said. "And they are from the Caribbean." The student gamely sang a line from a Rihanna song: *"And you got me like oh what you want from me?"* The classroom erupted with laughter.

Lila quieted the class. "Yes, Rihanna is from Barbados and Nicki Minaj is from Trinidad. But this course is not about singers from the Caribbean. This course is a survey of literature by writers from the Caribbean. You mentioned Jamaica, Trinidad, Barbados. I want to talk to you about St. Lucia. Do any of you know why I want to talk about St. Lucia in a Caribbean Literature course?"

No one spoke. The young man in the third row sank deeper into his seat, his iPhone mere inches from his nose.

Lila pulled out *Omeros* from her briefcase and read lines from Chapter 1:

> *the dawn breeze salted him coming up the grey street*
> *past sleep-tight houses, under the sodium bars*
>
> *of street-lamps, to the dry asphalt scraped by his feet;*
> *he counted the small blue sparks of separate stars.*

Someone coughed loudly. Lila looked up. She had been fighting back tears. They had come without warning, unexpectedly. When? Was it *the dawn breeze salted him*? Some mornings, mostly the days after a storm when the scent of the salt-sea air was strongest, she would leave her house and walk to the edge of the water. *The dawn breeze salted him*. It salted her too. At night, she too had counted the small blue sparks of separate stars.

A man in the back spoke before she could find her speaking voice, her vocal cords still twanging with the rhythms of Walcott's hexameter. "*Omeros*," he said. "It is Walcott's epic poem. It's about the struggles and joys of the common fishermen Walcott knew on his island. It is the odyssey of Caribbean people, from Africa to the

Middle Passage to the slave trade; it traces the waning days of European colonization."

Silence. Not a sound, not even the scratch of a pen or pencil on paper, not the tap of keys on a laptop. No one was taking notes.

Clive. Clive Lewis. It was he who had spoken. It was her first day. She was not prepared to talk about the slave trade or colonization, words that triggered anxiety, guilt, and, in some, automatic reminders of America's original sin. She didn't want to frighten them, push them into their defensive corners.

She met his eyes. He mouthed, *Sorry.* Then just as quickly as he appeared, he disappeared.

She had to get control of her class. "Yes," she said, "I just read to you from Walcott's epic *Omeros.* Have any of you heard of *The Iliad*?" A few hands shot up. "Well, in a way, *Omeros* is Walcott's *Iliad*." She fought against the voice in the back of her head that had begun to taunt her. Walcott's *Iliad*? Did Walcott appropriate Homer? Hadn't her essay denounced the appropriation of Caliban's island? It was a tropical isle like hers Caliban spoke of, not some place where the air was cold for months on end, but an isle where the air was sweet, smelling of the rich earth, where the noises of a thousand instruments were the melodies of singing birds and the snapping of branches from flowering plants, not frigid winds whistling through leafless trees.

She was aware that the students were watching her. She cleared her throat and began again: "The sea in Walcott's poem is not Homer's Mediterranean; it is the Caribbean Sea. Achille is not Achilles; he is a common fisherman in St. Lucia."

"So Walcott stole Homer's story?" It was the young female student who had sung the line from a Rihanna song.

Her question unnerved Lila. "Walcott did not *steal* Homer's story," she said firmly. "*Omeros* is Walcott's tribute to Homer. It is Walcott's story about the history of his people, the history of Caribbean people. His heroes, tragic and triumphant, are fishermen whose lives are at the mercy of the sea."

A redheaded young man in gray sweatpants and a T-shirt with the college's name emblazoned on the front unfolded his legs and waved his hand. "Will we be reading that big book?" he asked, pointing to the volume of *Omeros* Lila had placed on her desk. It *was* a big book, more than three hundred pages of hexameters, a Herculean feat for Walcott, more than a challenge for even the most ambitious reader of Caribbean literature.

The student was rude, disrespectful, but mostly he seemed bored. She had bored them all. And on the first day!

She had been defensive. It was not Walcott she had been defending; it was herself, her essay. The student had rescued her. "No, oh no," she said, quickly recovering her composure. "I just brought it to tell you about Walcott and to read a couple of lines."

The relief from the class was audible and the tension that had begun to build between Lila and the student evaporated.

Laughter. Lila pulled out Merle Hodge's novel *Crick, Crack Monkey* from her briefcase. "As you can see, it's a slim book." She fanned out the pages of the novel.

Not a few of the students sighed with relief. And

so began Lila's first day at Mayfield College. The young woman who sang the Rihanna song had probably asked her question innocently, though it was also possibly malicious, yet she had caused Lila to wonder if Robert had been right. Perhaps she needed to rethink her thesis on appropriation.

9

She heard the knock on her office door. "Come in," she said, "the door is unlocked."

He entered with his hands in the air and his eyes downcast. "Guilty as charged. I apologize."

"Sit, sit," she said, indicating the chair in front of her desk. She did not get up.

"I was waiting for you in the courtyard and then I thought, *Why not pop in her class? I could learn something.*"

"It seems there was nothing for you to learn. You knew it already," she said without emotion. She shuffled some papers on her desk.

"Your reading," he said. "It moved me."

He was biting his lower lip, staring at his hands. *The dawn breeze salted him.* She was moved too. Did he see when tears welled in her eyes?

"Walcott is my favorite poet," he said.

"Where does a man from Mayfield learn about Walcott?" she asked.

"I live here, but I also live and work in New York. Brooklyn."

"And that is where you learned about Walcott?"

"It's the home of Caribbean people, Brooklyn. But I didn't need to go there to learn about Walcott. When he won the Nobel Prize, I wanted to know why, so I picked up *Omeros*. Ever since then, I've been a fan." He

grinned. "True, I've had to read each line twice to understand what he's saying. And I miss a lot, I guess. But
he can write! Every line is like music. He amazes me. He
touches my soul." His blue eyes penetrated hers.

"The passage I read—"

"It must have reminded you of home," he said.

"Yes. Home."

"So will you forgive me?"

She had forgiven him already, and not only because
he came to her aid when she needed him, but now because he thought the way she did about Walcott, the
way she did about the power of literature.

He seemed to sense that she had relented. "So, shall
we go to the café I told you about?"

She could feel his eyes on her as she began gathering her class notes on her desk. She did not like that
he made her feel nervous, flustered. She should tell him
that what he did was disrespectful. She was teaching a
class and he had interrupted her.

"You promised," he said.

She silently stuffed her notes into her briefcase.

"Don't you want to know about the shooting?" he
asked.

This got her attention. "A professor was killed," she
said, trying to modulate her voice to disguise her curiosity. *He knows the woman.*

"Come," he said, and rose from his chair. "Let's have
tea and crumpets."

"Tea and crumpets?" She had been closing her briefcase, fully intending to go to the café with him. Now she
sat back down.

"A joke," he said. "Just a joke. Will you forgive me?"

"A second time," she said. "Do you go around saying things just to ask for forgiveness?"

"It's you," he said. "You make me act silly and I'm not a silly man."

"So what do you call your remark about tea and crumpets?"

"Stupid," he said. "Silly."

"We take such remarks seriously. Colonialism was not a joke to us."

"Forgive me?"

In the café she explained. "They, the British, had tea and crumpets, but we served them. We don't like reminders of those days of servitude."

"I know," he said. "I should have been more sensitive."

"You should have known our history better. You say you like Walcott. Maybe you need to reread him."

"Forgi—"

"Not again. This isn't about whether I forgive you or not. It's about *you*. It's about you doing the hard work, putting yourself in our place, seeing the effects of colonialism from our point of view." She had not meant to be so harsh. The words had spilled out from her mouth spontaneously. He seemed like a decent man, with good intentions. After all, he was the one who brought up the slave trade and colonialism on the first day of her class when she was hesitant (afraid?) of the students' response.

"Every time I am around a beautiful woman, I get tongue-tied," he said. "I say stupid things, I make silly jokes, and what I really want to say is how much I admire her. *Like* her." He lowered his voice. "I like you, Lila."

They were sitting opposite each other. She picked up the menu card, looked at it, put it down, and placed her left hand over it. Even if he tried, he could not miss the diamond shining on her finger.

"I'm engaged," she said.

"Did I say another stupid thing?"

"I love my fiancé. His name is Robert."

"Lucky man."

"I'm the lucky one."

This silenced him. He picked up the menu card. "So, shall we order?"

Over tea and sweet rolls—for he ordered tea too, though she was certain he drank coffee—she took the chance to ask him about the woman. How did he know her? He brought his hand to his mouth and twisted his lips. They were friends from high school, he said. Lila waited for more. He slid his hand down his chin and began again. He lost touch with her when he took a job in Brooklyn, he said, but recently she began communicating with him again. "Ron knew her too," he said abruptly.

"The chair of my department, Dr. Campbell, gave me the impression that she was a stranger to Ron," Lila said. "She said Dr. Brown, Ron, just happened to be at the restaurant. He was in the wrong place at the wrong time."

"He was in the right place all right," Clive said bitterly. "Adriana would have died if Ron Brown had not been there when he was."

"That's her name?"

"Adriana Sorkin." He looked down on his hands. "And Ron didn't only just know her. They were lovers."

Lila was stunned. "A white woman?" And yet why

should she have been stunned? Interracial romantic relationships were common on her island. Her father was the son of a white woman who was married to a man whose mother was Black and whose father was white. But Terrence said that Ron had wanted to warn her that there were perils to being in a country where you are a minority, where you are Black and the majority of the people are white. "Did anyone know this?"

"I expect your Dr. Carter would have known they were lovers," Clive said.

"Terrence?" Lila's eyes widened. Terrence had not given her the slightest hint that he knew about Ron's relationship with the woman lying on the sidewalk.

"That would be my guess. Adriana told me Ron was best friends with Dr. Carter."

"Best friends?"

"Dr. Carter, Terrence, may not have met her, but most likely he knew about her."

"Did other people know?"

"It was a secret. Adriana told me Ron didn't want anyone to know. She called me a few weeks ago. She said she was in trouble."

"Drugs," Lila said and averted her eyes.

"How did you know?"

"I heard when the police called for naloxone. Robert . . ." She glanced at him. "My fiancé." They would talk, they would have tea, but she wanted no more of *I like you, Lila*.

"Heroin." Bitterness lingered in his voice. "She was injecting it in her veins."

"Robert told me they give naloxone to save a drug addict who has overdosed."

"If Ron didn't keep her alive, it would have been too late for the naloxone," Clive said.

"He was blowing air into her mouth."

"Her lungs had collapsed."

"But how? How did this happen to her? Mrs. Lowell said she is a good woman. She comes from an old Mayfield family. Well respected."

"I'll tell you how," Clive said. "It's an epidemic everyone pretends doesn't exist." He grimaced. "And then poor Adriana. She *is* a good woman. Maybe because of Adriana they will look up and see what's in front of their eyes."

"The police thought Ron was hurting her."

"He was a Black man with his mouth on the mouth of a white woman. People will prefer to blame him, but Adriana was not well. Ron wanted to help her."

They were silent. Clive sat up in his chair and put his elbows on the table, his hands forming an arch under his chin. Lila toyed with the string of her spent tea bag in her empty cup.

"More tea?" Clive asked, and reached for the metal jar on the table. "Cold." He beckoned the waitress. "Hot water!" He glanced at Lila who frowned disapprovingly. "Please," he said to the waitress. "Could we have more hot water, please?" The frown on Lila's forehead disappeared.

"It was a pharmaceutical drug, OxyContin," Clive said, turning back to Lila. "She became addicted to it."

"To a pharmaceutical drug?" Lila knew about heroin, cocaine. Those mind- and body-killing drugs had already put a stranglehold on scores of young people on her island. Robert blamed America. In the good old days, he said, people on their island smoked weed, ganja, marijuana. It relaxed them after a hard day's work. They smoked, they drank, they caroused with friends, went to bed, woke up the next morning and did the same thing all over again. He said the Indian cane cutters in the cane fields would roll ganja cigars that were fatter and longer than tobacco-filled cigars. Now in some parts of their quiet island, men and women thin as rails nod in corners, their brains addled.

The Caribbean was the strainer. The drugs were shipped from Central America to the Caribbean, repackaged, and sent to the US. Not long ago, a twenty-foot container with cocaine packed in grapefruit juice cans arrived in Norfolk, Virginia. There was no follow-up, or if there was, no one in the Caribbean knew. Nobody was arrested.

"OxyContin at first," Clive said. "Eventually heroin. But that addiction begins with pharmaceutical drugs like OxyContin." He threw up his hands and laughed. "The drugs are in our medicine cabinets. At home. Imagine!" The laughter left his lips; it had never reached his eyes. "Greedy doctors prescribe the pills that greedier pharmaceutical companies sell to them. The more prescriptions the doctors write, the more the pharmaceutical companies reward them. Money flows and patients get addicted. Some die." He chewed his lip. "I guess Adriana was one of the lucky ones. She didn't die."

Ron died for her. But Lila kept the words in the back of her throat.

Clive looked again in the direction of the kitchen where the waitress had disappeared.

"She'll be back with the water soon," Lila said.

"Sorry." Clive crossed his legs. "Sometimes they take too long."

"Do you need to leave? Because . . ."

"No. Not at all. It's . . ."

"What?"

He uncrossed his legs. "She used to be pretty successful, you know." He picked at the menu card lying on the table. "Or so I was told."

"By her parents?"

"No. I hardly knew her parents." He flattened his hand on the menu. "I was in a bar in Brooklyn. Having a little too much to drink, I'm afraid. One of Adriana's friends came up to me and said I should set a better example for her friend. She knew both of us. I used to date Adriana. But that was a long time ago. We were teenagers then."

The waitress returned with the hot water and new tea bags. "I got it for you." Clive pointed to the metal jar. "I've had enough."

"Thanks." She was conscious of Clive's eyes following her movements as she poured the water into her cup and dunked the tea bag up and down. "What did she do?" she asked, redirecting Clive's attention. "You said she was successful."

"The friend said Adriana was a VP for some big department chain stores. She was the principal buyer for ladies' clothes. That was Adriana. Always fashionable. The best-dressed girl in high school. Anyhow, her friend told me that Adriana had become a lush. An alcoholic. I couldn't believe it. Then her friend filled me in on what had happened. Adriana lost that big job. You know, brick and mortar is out of style these days. Online. That's how everybody buys stuff. Well, it seemed losing that job was a hard blow for Adriana. Her friend said she got depressed, despondent."

"Couldn't she find another job?"

Clive shrugged. "That's what I said. But her friend said Adriana couldn't get over losing that job. She began drinking. Wine at first, then whiskey. Straight."

"She was having an affair with Ron. Couldn't he help her?"

"As I understood it, the two things happened at the same time: she lost her job and the affair ended."

"Maybe if Ron hadn't ended—"

"Turned out she was the one who broke up with Ron." Clive scratched his forehead. "Nah. That's not accurate. From what her friend told me, Adriana had put the question to him. You know: the *big* question."

"She wanted him to marry her."

"Not exactly. She was tired of the secrecy. She wanted to bring their affair into the open. So she gave him an ultimatum. Either her or his friends. Choose." He grinned. His teeth glittered. "I don't know why women do that. Men hate ultimatums."

"So she stopped seeing him?"

"*He* stopped seeing *her*."

"Was that when Adriana called you?" Lila sipped her tea. Steam rose past her cheeks and shaded her eyes. *An ultimatum. Was that the mistake I made too? Was that why Kenton left me? Marry me. Don't go to Africa.*

"We texted for a while," Clive said. "She told me she had the alcohol under control. It was headaches she was fighting now. Blinding headaches, she said. I told her she should see a doctor. Famous last words."

"You gave her good advice."

"I was in Brooklyn most of the time, but I promised to come see her. My God," he murmured and rubbed his eyes. "OxyContin. That's what the doctor I sent her to gave her."

"You told her to see a doctor. You didn't tell her which doctor. You didn't recommend—"

"It's all the same. I should have known better when she told me she was taking OxyContin. She said it helped. The headaches went away. There were times when she felt nothing. *Nothing*. There's a clue for you." He laughed.

"You couldn't have known," Lila said.

"Then the headaches came back." He spoke seriously now, his voice heavy with sadness. "I think by the time Adriana called me to tell me she was in trouble, she was already addicted to heroin. The OxyContin wasn't helping. Or maybe her doctor had a twinge of conscience and wouldn't renew her prescription. Her migraines were excruciating. Worse than before, she told me. She was spiraling down." He inhaled and when he released his breath, he said, his eyes cast downward, "I knew about the OxyContin, but I didn't know she was injecting heroin."

"How could you?"

"I was supposed to meet her at the restaurant. I came too late. The ambulance had already taken her away. Then I saw you . . ."

"I'm so grateful for your help. I can't thank you enough."

"Not necessary."

"And Ron? Did Ron just happen to be there?"

"I don't know. After I dropped you off at Mrs. Lowell's, I heard some people say that Ron was her supplier. That was a lie. He had nothing on him. No drugs, no pills, no heroin. There were no needles in his pockets, no weapons. No gun."

"I think it was heartache," Lila said.

"Heartache?"

"If you love someone and you lose them, the pain can be more devastating than any physical pain you suffer. You can lose all desire to keep on living. I'm not sure losing her job caused Adriana all those headaches. Maybe it was losing Ron. Maybe heartache caused her to take more and more pills to dull her pain."

She was thinking of those weeks when she could not sleep. When she could not eat after Kenton chose Africa over her.

Her grandmother took her to the doctor, but the doctor did not give her OxyContin, and she did not take cocaine or heroin to dull her pain. Her grandmother's love, her patience, her prayers pulled her out of the darkness, and slowly, day by day, she recovered. Work was her salvation. Time and work. She taught classes at the university, she read, she wrote essays. Then Robert came into her life.

10

"Heartache?" Robert scoffed. Foolishly, she had called him. Foolishly, for she could have guessed his reaction.

"Adriana must have called Ron and she was waiting for him at the restaurant," she said. "She fell into his arms when he came toward her. Maybe he didn't return her embrace. Maybe he didn't want to give her hope that they would be back together again. When she slumped down to the pavement, he would have seen she couldn't breathe. He tried, but he couldn't save her."

"It's the hypocrisy I object to," Robert said. "That's why I'm telling you, Lila, you should stay out of America's racial problem. You don't understand them and neither do I. I mean those Black footballers and Black basketball players would have kids imitating them with their raised fists shouting 'Black Power,' but what they really want is white power. *White women.* Look how many of them marry white women. The richer they are, the more likely their wives are white."

Lila knew the argument. It wasn't only the rich Black football and basketball players who married white women. On her island, her young Black female students worried about their chances of finding mates who were their intellectual peers and had the potential to earn sufficient income to give them a comfortable life, a nice house, vacations, a good education for their children. They would take bets, naming a successful Black man and asking each other to guess whether his wife was Black or white. It seemed even on online dating sites, Black women were the least likely to secure a date. Where white men almost exclusively chose white women on those sites, Black men showed no particular partiality to women of their color. "They make us feel unattractive," one student had told her. "They devalue us. It's as if we're not pretty enough, good enough. A woman wants to think of herself as beautiful, even if she's not. When they choose us, we feel beautiful. When they don't, our confidence plummets."

Her students loved her; she could have pointed out that she would not exist, would not be there to teach them, if a Black man had not had a child with a white woman or a Black woman with a white man. She was the offspring of generations of sexual partners both Black and white. Robert too could have no objections to intermarriage. His mother was Irish, his father both Chinese and African.

"Ron was dishonest," Robert said. "Wasn't it his friend Terrence who warned you that things are different in America because colored people are in the minority?"

"Black people," Lila said.

Robert ignored her. "Didn't he say colored people are oppressed in America?"

Black men are an endangered species. That was what Terrence said and Gail began weeping. Now Ron was dead, Terrence's prediction having literally come to pass. But Lila could not judge Ron as harshly as Robert felt free to do. She believed in love. She believed that true love was possible even between people who do not share the same cultures, who belong to different religions, different ethnicities, different social classes. She believed that our common humanity binds us. She believed that love depends on the sharing of like minds, on like notions of morality, of good and evil, on our commitment to those ethical values that make us human: compassion, empathy, justice. Ron may have found in Adriana a companion with whom he could share his innermost feelings. A soul mate. Yet Lila had to admit to herself that it troubled her that when Adriana asked Ron to make their relationship public, he refused.

"I think Ron loved Adriana and she loved him," Lila said.

"Well, did he?" Robert asked. "Did he love her?"

"Ron probably just didn't have the courage to face up to the criticism from his friends," she said.

"Oh, it would have been a contradiction men like him could handle," Robert said. "A case of having your cake and eating it too."

"They would have ostracized him."

"I wouldn't be too sure," Robert returned.

She had not expected she would become defensive. But Robert was right: it was not her fight. Still, Lila was increasingly convinced that Adriana had despaired, she lost all hope; she saw no reason for living. OxyContin might ultimately have led Adriana to heroin, but it was Ron's rejection of her that most likely caused her to take a faster route, a more direct route to bury the pain she could no longer withstand.

How lucky she was, Lila thought, that she had her grandmother, she had friends who comforted her when

Kenton left her. For who knows what could have happened to her? She could not envision that she would have turned to heroin, but there was worse. It was not unheard of that in deep despair people took their own lives.

"If Ron could, he probably would not have fallen in love with Adriana," she said to Robert.

Robert laughed. "You are such a romantic, Lila. People don't fall in love. Love is not like an accident that just happens to you. It starts with like. People who like each other grow to love each other."

"And can't you say the same for Ron? That he liked Adriana?"

"We have a will, Lila. Even if we like something, we can walk away from it if it's against our convictions. Ron could have walked away."

"What about love?"

"If the love is genuine, it's because you have already chosen. You don't walk away."

There was a hardness in his voice that frightened Lila, but the moment passed as swiftly as it had seized her heart. "I think it's possible, really possible, that Ron was in love with Adriana," she said.

"Then he should not have cared what anyone said. He should have married her."

In bed that night, Lila wondered whether Robert's comment was intended as a swipe at her. She should not have cared what anyone thought of her marriage to a divorced man. Her grandmother's opinion should not matter if she were truly in love with Robert.

11

It had only been two weeks since Ron Brown was killed and it seemed as if collectively the citizens of the town of Mayfield had amnesia.

As Lila made her way down Main Street to the college, Mayfield appeared to her as the quintessential quiet New England village she had read about in travel books: steepled churches, white picket fences, houses painted in reserved New England colors, the same colors that in tropical countries could dazzle the eye, but here the reds were brick-colored, the yellows almost mustard, the greens mirroring forest firs. Along tree-lined streets, couples walked hand in hand with their well-behaved, rosy-cheeked children. One would be hard-pressed, she thought grimly, to convince a stranger that just days before, long thick trails of blood had been scrubbed clean in front of the restaurant where a relatively young Black man, a professor at Mayfield College, was shot dead by the police while astride a white woman who had OD'd on heroin.

But it was a warm day even for early fall, and nothing spoiled the Disney fairy-tale image Mayfield presented. The leaves on the trees were already turning into brilliant reds, russets, and golds, and the lake at the end of the street glittered gloriously in the brilliant sunshine. Lila passed the restaurant where the shooting had taken place. It was bustling with lunch customers. Through the large front windowpanes she could see them laughing and chatting happily over stuffed plates and frosted glasses. (No alcohol in the iced glasses; the good town of Mayfield did not permit alcohol in the middle of the day.) There were others, though, who she could tell were not at ease, not comfortable with what had happened in their town, in front of the restaurant. She could see them bent over their plates, from time to time glancing at the entrance as if expecting something ominous to appear. The ghost of Ron Brown perhaps? Or perhaps Adriana, limp, pale-faced, about to slide down on the pavement before that man had the misfortune to catch her, and then, even more disastrously (for him, that is), to straddle her? Lila shook her head. Too few of them seemed troubled. Most of Mayfield had already dismissed the shooting and the near death of a woman destroyed by heroin as a rarity, something that was very unlikely to happen again. It was an event that deserved to be forgotten, and their gaiety reassured them of the rightness of their decision.

But what about the students? Had they forgotten too? Along the narrow paved path toward the cafeteria, which was in the building directly opposite to the academic wing of the college, Lila saw no evidence that the attitude of the students was any different from that of the townspeople. In the quad, they were sitting on the lawn clustered in circles, chatting animatedly with each other. Some students turned their heads toward her when she passed by, but the second she caught their eyes and was about to raise her hand in greeting, they turned back. They lowered their voices too, for the peals of laughter she had heard moments before suddenly quieted. Then she saw the banner. It was stretched across the wall at the entrance of the cafeteria, next to the student notice board: *Black Lives Matter*. The words were written in large black letters on a white sheet. Standing in front of the banner was a group of students, male and female, wearing black sweatshirts, the hoods drawn over their heads. When she reached the top step, they stood at attention, one hand raised defiantly in a fist. "Black Lives Matter!" one of them chanted.

Lila smiled nervously. What was she expected to do, to say? Was she to return the salute? She had seen other faculty pass through the door before her. The students had not saluted them.

A loud voice called out her name. Elaine was hurrying toward, her colorful caftan fluttering like wings behind her. "Come, come sit with us." She waved at the students standing by the door. They raised their fists acknowledging her. "Black Lives Matter!" they chanted in unison.

"There are two of us. You make three." Elaine winked. "Get your food and join us at our table."

Us. She was part of us. The students in front of the Black Lives Matter banner had recognized her. They had drawn her into their protest, she and she alone, not the white faculty who had entered the cafeteria just before she did.

She remembered a game she played as a child and the song that went with it:

There's a brown girl in a ring, tra la la la la
There's a brown girl in a ring, tra la la la la

There's a brown girl in a ring, tra la la la la
And she sweet like a sugar and a plum plum plum . . .

On her island she was a brown girl, sweet like a sugar and a plum plum plum.

She had said to Robert she was Black. Did that mean she was not a brown girl? That her nationality did not count? That it was more important to be Black than to be a Caribbean woman?

Robert had called her back later that night. "So am I Black too?" he asked.

"In America you are Black if there is African blood in your ancestry."

"And what if there's more Caucasian blood?"

She was silent.

"So *they* will define me. Is that it, Lila? I must abdicate my right to define myself?"

She had no answer to give him.

Lila bought a sandwich and a bottle of juice and brought them to the table. Terrence was there, sitting opposite to Elaine. Lila was to learn that this was the Black table, reserved for Black faculty and their guests. No one had stipulated it so. It was just the way it was, Elaine said. There was a tacit agreement: the white faculty did not sit at that table at lunchtime.

Robert had told her he had read that Martin Luther King Jr. said that the most segregated hour of Christian America is eleven o'clock on Sunday morning. And now segregated lunch tables! Perhaps, Lila thought, Robert was not wrong: she did not know America.

"Those were Ron's students." Terrence jerked his head toward the door. "They've been planning to hang that banner for some time now, but the dean refused to give them permission. He called them agitators." He cleared a space for Lila at the table next to him.

"How did they convince the dean to let them put it up?" Lila asked as she took a seat.

"The father of one of the students is a lawyer. He's connected to the American Civil Liberties Union. The dean knew better than to come up against the ACLU." He grinned. There wasn't a hint of levity in his smile. "Then Ron . . . Then after Ron . . ." He was breathing easier now. "The dean balked for a couple of days, but eventually the students got to put up the Black Lives Matter banner. Like us, they're waiting for the coroner's report. But they know. *We* know."

"When will you get the results?" Lila asked.

"The coroner should release Ron's body soon. It should be a slam dunk. He was riddled with bullets. He didn't have a gun."

"It will be a big funeral," Elaine said.

"The trial is what I'm waiting for," said Terrence. "I want to see how the police will explain this one."

Lila looked out of the window. Ron's students were walking down the steps. Terrence followed her eyes. "They'll be back again," he said. "I hope Mayfield will be ready. If they exonerate those police officers, I don't think the students will be silent."

"We'll see." Elaine pursed her lips.

Ron's students were no longer discernable among the other students now rushing to their classes, though there was one Lila noticed. Unlike those who had saluted her, he had not removed his hood; it was still covering his head. A young woman stopped him and seemed to playfully remove it. Long strands of dark hair tumbled down the sides of the hood. The young woman reached inside and pulled out his ponytail, then flicked it in the air. Lila could vaguely see the dark outlines of a tattoo curling up his pale neck.

"So how are your classes going?"

Terrence's voice jolted her back to the table. She had not seen him since they had lunch together the previous week. "The students are interesting," she said, and bit into her sandwich.

Terrence grinned. "Interesting? Is that all you can say?"

"Well, they have an uncomplicated idea of the Caribbean."

"If it's not in America or about America, they don't probe too much," said Elaine.

"They know the songs. Bob Marley. Rihanna," said Lila.

"I'm sure you'll let them know there's more than songs," said Elaine.

"They know about the drugs. What's going on in Jamaica with drugs. On my island too."

Terrence lowered his eyes. The muscles on his temple twitched. "She was on heroin." There was no need to say who. "It's a big problem in Vermont," he said. "They take painkillers. OxyContin. When that doesn't work, they inject heroin."

Elaine's lips quivered. "Ron was courageous."

"Foolish," Terrence struck back angrily. "You see a white woman in trouble, call the police. Don't get involved."

"She might have died," Lila said.

"Ron died." Terrence's eyes met hers. *If looks could kill*—the expression was made real for Lila in that moment. She wanted to say something, but her tongue was glued to the roof of her mouth. With great effort she managed to tear her eyes away from Terrence's.

"How's your sandwich, Lila?" Elaine asked. She shook her head at Terrence signaling him to drop the line he seemed intent in pursuing.

Terrence grunted, but complied. "I always make my own sandwiches," he said. "I don't trust what they put in the prepackaged ones."

"He's paranoid," Elaine said.

"Oh, I don't think they'll put anything in it to make me sick. That's not what I'm talking about. I don't like pickles and sometimes the label on the prepackaged sandwiches say no pickles and then I bite into it . . ."

"And pickles!" Elaine threw up her hands, teasing him. Terrence smiled reluctantly.

"I bought this one," Lila said. "Turkey and cheese."

"Turkey and cheese," Terrence intoned. "Safe choice."

For some reason that was not clear to Lila, it seemed to her that Terrence was speaking about more than her sandwich. *Safe choice?* Was he implying that all her choices were safe? She had left her island, her position at her university, family and friends, to come to Mayfield. She had taken the chance that Robert may not be waiting for her when she returned.

"So I take it you've met Dr. Campbell," Terrence said.

"She came to Mrs. Lowell's house. That's where I'm staying."

"At Mrs. Lowell's, huh?"

"She's a friend of Dr. Campbell's."

"But you'd have preferred your own apartment, wouldn't you?"

"If it were convenient," Lila said. "But Dr. Campbell explained that there's only one apartment building in the town."

"And it's fully occupied, right?" Terrence and Elaine exchanged glances.

"Yes. That's what she wrote to me in her e-mail."

"And you believed her?" Terrence said.

"Why shouldn't I have?"

Elaine cleared her throat and glared at Terrence, who rocked back in his chair. "If that's what Dr. Campbell said, that must be how it is."

"It was kind of her to find a place for me to stay."

Terrence steadied his chair. "Dr. Campbell was smart to hire you."

"All due to you," Lila said.

"All due to *you*," Terrence countered, pointing his finger at her. "Your essay is brilliant."

"You're kind to say so."

"It's the truth. But Dr. Campbell had other reasons for needing you in her department."

"Needing me?"

"I'm sure you know you are the only Black faculty there. Ron was encouraging students to demand that the college hire more Black faculty."

"You were too, Terrence," Elaine said, and stretched her arm across the table. Their fingers touched briefly.

Terrence sighed. "I was a follower, not the leader. Anyhow, Mary Campbell—the whole college really—is under pressure to do something about the lack of diversity on campus. Diversification!" he sneered. "It's the latest code word, but nothing will change. Sprinkle a few Black people in white neighborhoods, in white schools, and end of problem."

"Is that why—"

"Oh, we are proud to have you here with us at Mayfield, Lila," Elaine said quickly. "Lucky."

"We want more like you," Terrence said. "Many more." He glanced at the window. "They've left. *Black Lives Matter*. That was what Ron was teaching his students." He turned back to Lila. "You must have heard about Trayvon Martin and Eric Garner. Many others too. Now Ron's gone." He swiveled his head, his eyes taking in the people on the right and left of their table. "Look around you. Look at the people in the cafeteria, in the college, in the town. It's as if Ron's life did not matter. An e-mail! That's all the president of the college sent. An e-mail saying how sorry he was, how sad. Ron was in the wrong place at the wrong time: That's their defense. I don't know what Ron's students will do, or if anyone will join them, but I do know that if once again the police are not indicted for killing a Black man, it will be impossible to silence them."

12

Trayvon Martin and Eric Garner.

Even on her island, mothers were horrified. And frightened too. Trayvon Martin was holding a bag of Skittles—a sweetie, they would call a Skittle on her island.

He was just seventeen, a teenager. Minding his own business, probably humming the latest hip-hop song in his head, not thinking that there could be people who were watching him. And why should he be thinking that people would be watching him? He was returning to his father's home where he had left minutes before to go buy a bag of Skittles. Did it matter that he didn't live there with his father?

A man called out to him to stop. He turned around, saw it was a white man, turned back, and kept on walking. The man warned him again: "Stop!" Trayvon opened the bag and ate his Skittles.

Was the man infuriated, his sense of his entitlement, his power as a white man, dashed by Trayvon's attitude, his insouciance? Trayvon was wearing a blackish sweatshirt, dark gray, with the hood drawn over his head. Black boys—Black men—with hoodies covering their heads were troublemakers, criminals. He would show the Black boy with a hoodie that he didn't belong in this nice neighborhood where white people lived. Was that what that man was thinking?

At first the women on Lila's island faulted Trayvon. "Do teenagers ever listen to us? Big people don't like when they tell you to do something and you answer back with a fresh mouth."

But no one could answer the question: does it take bullets to stop a teenager who was fresh, rude to you?

After nerves calmed down, mothers reminded themselves that the fatal shooting of a Black boy by a self-described vigilante, protector of white property, did not happen on their island; it happened in America where the majority of the people are white. Here, on their island, it was unusual to find a white judge, a white lawyer, a white doctor, a white teacher, a white engineer, a white banker. More common in those professions were people who were Black or Indian or Chinese. Black people, dark-skinned people, lived in shacks, but Black people, dark-skinned people, also lived in big beautiful houses with perfumed gardens and manicured lawns. A Black boy in a hoodie with Skittles in his hand was just a Black boy in a hoodie with Skittles in his hand, maybe the son or relative of the people who own the big houses.

Two years later, Eric Garner, a Black man, was strangled to death by white police officers. He was standing on the pavement selling "loosies." The police had warned him several times that selling loose cigarettes was illegal. Eric Garner scoffed at them. Then on the afternoon of July 17, 2014, the police officers lost patience. They held him down; one of them put his arm across his neck in a chokehold. "I can't breathe," Eric Garner cried out seventeen times. Before he could cry out for the eighteenth time, all breath left his body. He was forty-three years old, a father of six children, one of them three months old.

Mothers, wives, sisters, grandmothers on Lila's island feared for their Black sons, Black fathers, Black husbands, Black brothers, Black uncles, Black cousins who had immigrated to America. Robert hadn't wanted Lila to go to America. "But at least you're not a Black man," he said.

No, Lila had not needed Terrence to remind her about Trayvon Martin and Eric Garner.

Terrence left the table first. He had to teach a class after lunch, he said. As he was leaving, he paused and wagged his finger at Lila. "You saved Dr. Campbell's ass."

"It's the truth," Elaine said when Terrence was gone.

"It's an opportunity for me," she said.

"I wish you could have come at a better time. You would have liked Ron," Elaine said.

"Dr. Brown sounds like he was a good man," Lila said. "Everyone seems to have loved him."

"Not *seems*. They . . . I . . ." Elaine's voice faltered slightly. "*We*," she said, assertively now. "We all loved him . . . Come. Let's go." She stood up. "I have a class too this afternoon, but I can walk a bit with you to where you're going."

Lila was headed to the college library. She wanted to find out more about the epidemic that had almost taken a young woman's life and put her protector in the morgue, a young Black professor with a brilliant future before him. Terrence said it was a big problem in Vermont. "I have some work to do in the library," Lila said.

"Then I'll walk with you there. My class is near enough."

When they parted, Elaine put her arms around Lila. "We are grieving," she said. "We are angry, but we are grieving. We loved Ron. I . . ." She couldn't finish; her voice cracked.

13

Lila was shocked. Nothing prepared her for what she read when she googled *opioid epidemic in Vermont* on the computer in the library. Children as young as eight addicted to heroin, more young people dead from opioid overdose than from traffic accidents and murders combined. Close to fifty babies out of a thousand births in Vermont born with symptoms of opioid exposure and the numbers were climbing. And the drugs were in their medicine cabinets! That was what Clive had said. On the web she found out that doctors were prescribing painkillers in huge quantities and at high levels of concentration. In the previous year in the US, doctors wrote close to three hundred million prescriptions for painkillers, enough for every man, woman, and child in America to have a bottle of pills. Their patients became addicted. When they couldn't get the painkillers, they turned to heroin and cocaine. Heroin and cocaine were cheaper than prescription drugs. They could get them on the streets for one-fifth the price of the legal drugs. There was plenty blame to go around: greedy pharmaceutical companies, greedy distributors who, though they knew that the quantities of OxyContin they delivered to small-town pharmacies tripled, even quadrupled the number of the people who lived there, continued delivering. Terrence had not exaggerated. Clive Lewis had not lied. Vermont was in the grip of an opioid crisis. And now a heroin and cocaine crisis loomed.

How did she not know this? In the American movies she had seen, in the American newspapers and magazines she had read, on the news from America piped into her home on TV, the drug addicts were African Americans. The jails were full of them: African Americans who had succumbed to crack, cocaine, heroin. Addicts, invariably Black, sleeping in the streets under cardboard boxes, nodding off in corners, hands held out begging for whatever you could give them: a dime, a quarter. Thin as scarecrows, their bellies sunk to their bones. But food was not what they craved. They would steal from their mothers for a fix. They would kill. Love and friendship counted for nothing. Better to sweep them off the streets. Better to lock them up.

She had not seen Black men nodding off in corners in Mayfield. Nor white men either. But if the report was right, there must have been white men and women in the throes of heroin addiction swaying like zombies on the streets of Mayfield.

How had she missed them? Was it that Mayfield had camouflaged their addicts with its fairy-tale image, directing her eyes to happy couples, happy children, flowers in whiskey barrels, houses built in the reassuring styles of prosperous times, a silvery lake shimmering under the sun, colorful sailboats?

And how had Mayfield not seen Adriana leaning against the front rails of the restaurant, her legs wobbling beneath her, her head drooping into her chest, her eyes glassy, empty like those of dead fish?

Lila clicked off the article she was reading. A Black man was dead; the white woman was alive, in the hospital, in rehabilitation.

There was a department meeting later in the afternoon, the first for Lila. Two minutes of silence. That was all they gave Ron. Two minutes and then a brief statement from Dr. Campbell. *Unfortunate circumstances.*

Someone offered that the woman was lucky. Ron had saved "the poor girl's" life.

Dr. Campbell demurred. Ron should have obeyed the police.

"But if he had left . . ." the professor who had spoken began again.

"*If,*" said Dr. Campbell. "But we are not here to discuss *if*. There's going to be a police investigation and I would advise everyone here to follow the example of our president. We don't want trouble on our campus. Our job is to maintain normalcy here at Mayfield. For our students, for their sake. An e-mail to all of them expressing condolence would be good. If one or two of your students want to say something, let them. But let it be short. No long treatises."

A chuckle rippled through the room. *Treatises? Students sent texts. They tweeted.*

"Afterward, resume your class as usual," Dr. Campbell said, then picked up her notepad. "Now for some good news. We have someone new among us. A distinguished professor from the University of the West Indies. Dr. Lila Bonnard. Stand up, Dr. Bonnard. Welcome!"

Applause.

Dr. Campbell glanced at her notepad and then over

to Lila. "Bonnard. A French name. I suppose your family comes from that long line of Frenchmen who went to the Caribbean to seek their fortune. Not so, Dr. Bonnard?"

Lila's throat tightened. She wanted to say, *The French who came to the Caribbean were slave owners*, but she kept her silence.

"They planted sugarcane and cocoa. Correct, Dr. Bonnard?"

African enslaved women and men did that backbreaking work for them, she would have said. But this was not the occasion or the place to give the history of her island. What she managed to say was, "My father was not a Frenchman. Like most of us in the Caribbean, he was mixed with many bloods. Including African."

Dr. Campbell reddened and turned to the faculty. "Dr. Bonnard comes to our small Mayfield College with exceptional qualifications," she said. "She has a PhD from Oxford University. She is recognized in academia as a major authority in Caribbean literature, particularly for her essays in her latest book."

Lila could feel blood swelling in her neck. *A major authority! Her latest book!* She had published only one book. She was good at what she did, but she was not exceptional. There were many scholars back on her island who had surpassed her accomplishments.

"And, of course, some of you already know why we were so interested in her work. It comes at a time when racial tensions are high in the country. Dr. Bonnard raises questions about appropriation that some of our students are grappling with. Her reference, as it is for all of us in the English Department, is the Great Books. She uses Shakespeare to make her argument. *The Tempest*. Admittedly, that play has been overanalyzed, and I would say in most cases erroneously so." She glanced at Lila, who looked away.

"The Caliban/Prospero relationship has been used and overused," Dr. Campbell continued. "Used foolishly to make all sorts of political arguments that I am certain Shakespeare never intended. But . . ." she was smiling slyly at Lila now, "Dr. Bonnard gives us a different insight. She praises Caliban for his lyricism and makes the argument that he is so much admired that the British now want to appropriate him."

Lila could hear whisperings and titters from the back of the room. *They're laughing at me!* "I don't think, Dr. Campbell, that one can say the British admire Caliban," she said. "It was not my intention to make that claim. I think those lines that begin 'Be not afeared' are some of the most beautiful lines that Shakespeare wrote. My point was that they belong to Caliban; they come from his voice."

"And I can speak for the rest of the faculty that we look forward to the opportunity to have you tell us more," Dr. Campbell said. "If I can arrange a meeting with our colleagues, would you be willing to discuss your thesis? It's about appropriation, isn't it?"

"Yes," Lila said. "I would be honored."

The faculty applauded again and the meeting proceeded without any more references to Lila's work or her presence at the college. There were announcements of achievements over the summer, more applause for faculty whose work had appeared in scholarly journals or who had secured contracts for future publications, applause too for faculty who had made presentations at conferences or had served on panels. Nothing was said about pedagogy or ways to improve teaching. Nothing more either about Ron, though when Lila was leaving the conference room, the professor who had challenged Dr. Campbell with *if* made his way over to her, shook her hand, and said, his eyes cast downward, "Ron was a good man. We need to end this. I'm so, so sorry."

And for a moment Lila wondered if his expression of sympathy was meant for Ron or for himself.

Back in her apartment in Mrs. Lowell's house, Lila opened the copy of James Baldwin's *Notes of a Native Son* her friend Ruth had given to her before she left her island for Mayfield. There was a passage about appropriation Ruth wanted her to read. "If you're going to talk about appropriation in America," she had said, "you need to know what one of America's foremost writers had to say on that topic."

Lila was expected to give a lecture on appropriation. Dr. Campbell's request was not an invitation she could decline; she did not have a choice.

Baldwin surprised her. He had published *Notes of a Native Son* in 1955, when he was twenty-one years old. In the first essay, "Autobiographical Notes," he reflects on the necessity for the writer to look back before he could write meaningfully about the present or the future, and he concludes that when he followed the line of his past, he did not find himself in Europe but in Africa. Referring to the great creations of Europe, Baldwin admits: "I had no other heritage which I could possibly hope to use . . . I would have to appropriate these white centuries, I would have to make them mine . . ."

Appropriate! Baldwin had used that exact word. If he had second thoughts about the inaccuracy of the term, he would have so indicated in the introduction of the new edition that appeared years later, in 1984, when he was sixty years old.

So her friend had disagreed with her. Her gift of Baldwin's book was intended as cautionary advice. For there was Baldwin, one of the most revered writers in America, an African American, giving his approval for the appropriation of art from a culture that was not his own.

Ruth had attached a Post-it note to the front page: *Tolstoy is the Tolstoy of the Zulus, so says Ralph Wiley.* It was Wiley's response to Saul Bellow, a Jewish American novelist who won the Nobel Prize in 1976. Bellow had famously asked: "Who is the Tolstoy of the Zulus?" Surely, Bellow had wanted to cast aspersions on the literary abilities of Black writers. And here, with her cautionary note, Ruth had given her Wiley's answer and more. Zulu writers, Black writers, are as talented as Tolstoy *and* the works of Tolstoy belong not only to the Russians, but, as Baldwin implied in his essay, also to us.

So why not Shakespeare? Why not those lyrical lines Shakespeare had given to Caliban? Didn't they also belong to those Englishmen in top hats who recited them at the Olympics?

Lila closed the book. Soon she would have to prepare her lecture. There was much for her to think about.

14

Lila heard the news accidentally that the coroner had finally released Ron's body. She was walking down the pathway from the academic building, exhausted from teaching the class she had promised on Merle Hodge's *Crick, Crack Monkey*. The student who had tried to derail her by smearing the entire island of Jamaica as a haven for drugs had challenged her again.

"What sort of language is that?" the young man had complained. Lila consulted her seating chart. His name was Oliver Mason, perhaps handed down from British ancestors whose people were still the largest white population in Vermont.

Lila explained that the main character spoke in the language of her Caribbean island. "But is it English?" Oliver persisted.

"It is a fusion of the English language and all the other languages of the people who once lived on the islands," Lila explained. "It may not be what one would call Standard English, or a standard European language, but it is spoken by everyone on the island."

"Oh, it's a dialect," said the girl sitting next to Oliver. "A sort of patois."

"Nation language. The legitimate language of the people who live there," Lila said.

The effort it took to redirect the class to the themes

of the novel drained Lila's energy, and when the class ended, she was glad she did not have much farther to walk before she would be home, at Mrs. Lowell's, able to relax in her room. As she approached the end of the pathway, however, she was stopped.

She had noticed the group of students huddled together talking excitedly. She recognized them, or, rather, she recognized the student with the long dark ponytail. They were all wearing the same black sweatshirts but with the hoods draped over their upper backs. The student with the dark ponytail turned around when he saw her. "Black Lives Matter," he said in a low voice.

She intended simply to acknowledge them and wish them good day—she did not want to be drawn into their political protest—but the student had more to say.

"Did you hear?" He came closer to her. She could see the black tattoo curling up his neck.

"Hear what?" she asked.

"The coroner released Dr. Brown's body. The body is now on its way to a funeral parlor in Brooklyn." He handed her a crumpled piece of paper. "Just the facts," he said bitterly. "But the facts as the coroner saw them. Not the real facts. Not about how Dr. Brown was unarmed and the police killed him." And he recounted the coroner's facts for Lila: Four bullets had penetrated Dr. Brown's body. One went through his right leg, one through his groin on the right side, one into his chest below his heart. The bullet to his head was the one that killed him. "We'll be going to the funeral," the young man announced, sweeping his arm over the rest of the group. "All of us."

Lila nodded.

"So I expect we'll see you at the funeral. Right, Professor?"

Right. Lila said the word quietly, in her head. Aloud she said, "I'm glad you'll be going. Dr. McLean told me you were Ron Brown's students."

"He was the best," the ponytailed student said.

So, so . . . Why couldn't she answer? Why did she go silent when the student said he expected she would be there?

"I hope you don't plan to go," Robert said when she called him. "There'll be trouble in New York. It would be best if you stayed in Mayfield." There was a long pause on the phone when Lila did not respond. Then Robert spoke again, this time his tone stern, demanding. "You didn't tell anyone that you were there when Ron got shot, did you, Lila?"

"Elaine saw me."

"But did you tell anyone else? The police?"

"I went straight to Mrs. Lowell's."

"With that man? Clive what's-his-name?"

"Clive Lewis. He helped me."

"So he saw the whole thing too."

"I'm not sure. I think he came afterward. After Ron was shot."

"Well, Dr. McLean, Elaine, saw. So there's no need for you to get involved."

"She was on the other side of the street. Sitting on the pavement."

"What are you trying to say to me, Lila?" Robert raised his voice. "Are you trying to say that you were the only witness?"

"There had to be others. I'm just not sure Elaine or Clive Lewis saw what I saw."

"Lila, don't be foolish. Stay out of this."

Lila shut her eyes. The roar of bullets blasted through her ears. In her mind's eye, she saw the blood leaking out of Ron's skull and curling down the pavement. She saw his shirt, his pants soaked red, stuck to his limp body.

"I don't want you to go to the funeral," Robert said firmly.

"He was my age," Lila said.

"Don't go thinking he was just like you. You come from two different worlds."

"It was horrible," Lila said. "I saw. I told you I saw."

"You *think* you saw."

"He was trying to give the woman CPR." *Her lungs had collapsed. That's what Clive said.* "She could have died if Ron hadn't breathed into her mouth."

"You don't know that. Anyhow, I hope you didn't say that to anyone. I'm warning you, Lila." He stopped. Revising his words, he spoke gently now: "I'm saying this to you for your own good. You don't want to get wrapped up in that mess."

"*Mess?* A man died. My colleague. Or he would have been my colleague."

"He was a drug dealer."

"How can you say that, Robert?"

"It's all over the Internet. The woman . . . Adriana was waiting for him to give her a heroin fix."

"It's a lie. The people who wrote that, said that, are disgusting. Evil. Ron was a professor."

"Are you saying that because he was a professor, he

wasn't using heroin? Wake up, Lila. Don't be so naive. I'm telling you, don't go to the funeral. You don't know these people. You are not an American."

Late at night, she trolled the Internet again. Looking for what? That Terrence had exaggerated when he said Black men are an endangered species?

On a web page, draped in black, she found the names of the dead, listed one by one, all of them Black, men, women, children killed by police officers, all the dead unarmed.

So many names. So many more names to come, Terrence would tell her, his face mournful, eyes rimmed red. And she would wish she had reason to tell him he was wrong.

15

She looked everywhere for them, in the cafeteria, in the faculty conference room, in the library. She knocked on their office doors. No one answered. She asked people she had never spoken to, faculty from other departments, students rushing to class: "Have you seen Professor McLean, Professor Carter?" Some had seen them. One professor said early in the morning; another said just before lunch. No one saw them after lunch.

A student offered that as she was crossing the college parking lot, she saw them. Professor Carter was sitting in his car. It seemed he was waiting for someone. Then she saw Dr. McLean walking toward the car. "She was walking fast," the student said. "And she was pulling a small suitcase behind her."

"Eloping! They were eloping!" The student next to her clapped her hands, threw back her head, and laughed.

A calmer voice stopped her: "Dr. McLean always carries a small suitcase. It's for her books, you idiot."

Still, Lila worried. Did they leave without her?

She couldn't find Gail either. The receptionist in the bursar's office told her that Gail had called and she wouldn't be in today.

"Tomorrow?" Lila asked.

"Not for the rest of the week," the receptionist said.

She had time. Lila consoled herself with the likelihood that the funeral would be days away. The ponytailed student said Ron's body had left the coroner's office that morning. It was Wednesday. The earliest the funeral would take place would be Saturday.

She wanted to go; she had decided to go, so she kept looking for them, for Terrence, for Elaine, for Gail. She sent them e-mails, texts. She telephoned. No answer, not from the e-mails, not from the texts, not from the telephone calls. *Did they go to Brooklyn without me?*

16

She couldn't sleep. Even the house mocked her. Mrs. Lowell had long gone to bed, but all was not still. The old Victorian house creaked and groaned, and the windows shuddered each time the wind rose and blew against the glass panes. She did not belong, not here in this house, not in this country, not in this town, not where oak trees grew and leaves on giant trees changed colors from green to red and crumbled on the ground; not where soon winter will come and naked branches will be blanketed in white snow. She belonged on a warm-weather island where poui trees blossomed in vibrant yellows and pinks, and flamboyant and immortelle trees blanketed hills vermillion, a Caribbean island where winter never came and warm white sands ringed turquoise water. Never before had she felt lonelier, more dejected, more alienated. They had embraced her, welcomed her to Mayfield, had declared she was one of their own, and now they had separated themselves from her. Terrence, Elaine, Gail, all gone without her. What had happened to Ron was African American business, they seemed to imply, to be dealt with by African Americans.

Two more days to teach and then the weekend. They will be back on Monday, she told herself to quiet her anxiety. And when they returned, what would they say to her? What would she say to them?

Her class on Thursday proceeded as had her other classes. No one mentioned Ron Brown, not a whisper about the fatal shooting of one of their professors or a word about the woman who had OD'd. The debate about the language of some of the characters in Hodge's novel had subsided and new arguments began about whether or not Tee, the main character, would have been better off staying with her aunt in the country rather than going to the city to live with her maternal aunt.

"At least with her aunt in the city, she'd learn to speak proper English, not patois," a student said.

"Nation language," Lila reminded the student.

"Well, whatever. Her father's family are obviously uneducated and can do nothing to help her rise in the world. They live outside of the city, in a backward part of the island. But her mother's family live in the city, with all the advantages of city life. They have the money, they have class, and they are educated. They have much more to offer Tee. Yet Hodge seems to want us to believe that Tee would be happier with her paternal aunt, living in poverty. That seems implausible to me."

It was implausible to most of the other students too, but the class session was ending and Lila was feeling emotionally drained. So she decided to give them one more day to reassess their positions on Tee's choice. Perhaps by then they would also have reassessed their willingness to remain silent about the killing of their professor.

Then, on Friday, a student who had sat quietly in the back of the classroom all semester surprised her. At first the student gave no hint that she too could not bear the silence, the pretense; that she too had had enough.

She began by defending Tee's poor aunt, claiming that Tee's city aunt was snooty, that Tee was happier living with her aunt in a poor area because the people there loved her and accepted her for who she was. And then abruptly she pivoted. "We here in Mayfield do not accept people for who they are. We are prejudiced," she said. A low murmur ran through the classroom. "They may have class prejudice on Tee's island but we have race prejudice in our country."

Lila distinctly heard someone say, "Not in Mayfield."

"Yes, it's true," the student said, not backing down. "There's not much difference between us and Tee's snooty city aunt. We have racism here, in our backyard. In Mayfield."

Pages turned, the students flipping through Hodge's novel.

The student took a deep breath and continued: "Dr. Brown was a professor at our college. He was gunned down, here, in Mayfield. He was Black and the police who shot him were white."

"So?" a male student asked sarcastically.

"So, it's happening everywhere. That's what's so. Black men are being gunned down. Don't you read the newspapers? If you checked out the news on your phone instead of playing your silly games, you'd see what I'm talking about. When you are white, the police ask questions first. When you are a Black man, they shoot you first and then ask questions afterward."

Someone guffawed and mumbled under his breath, "Dead men tell no lies."

The student fastened her eyes on the young man. "Do you know what they are saying about us in Brooklyn? They are saying that we are racists, that we live in a racist town."

The only sounds were those of feet shuffling uncomfortably across the floor, the odd cough or clearing of the throat. Eyes shifted downward to opened books, or to the walls, anyplace but to the student or to the front of the room where Lila whispered to herself, "At last."

Sunday. She was not yet fully awake when her cell phone rang. It was Clive calling her. "I came back last night," he said.

"From the funeral?"

"Yes. I was there."

"They left without me."

"I know."

The phone went silent. Finally Lila said, "I looked for them. Everywhere. They were gone."

"Will you have breakfast with me?"

"I just got up."

"I can wait for you."

Another pause.

"Did you see them? Did you speak to them?"

"I saw them," he said. "Come. Have breakfast with me. I'll tell you about it."

She met him at the same café where they'd had lunch a few days earlier. His face was drawn, the lines around his mouth cut deeper. There was no light in his eyes; they were dull, sad.

She chose a table in a corner of the café. She didn't want to be seen. The funeral was yesterday. The students would know she hadn't gone. She'd been on her way to her class on Thursday morning when one of the young men who was with the group in the black hooded sweatshirts had asked her if she planned to cancel her classes. "Dr. McLean and Dr. Carter canceled their classes today and Friday," he said. "I think they left yesterday."

"Not today," she said, and she allowed him to assume that she would be at the funeral that weekend. But the young man and his friends would have gone to the funeral; they would know by now she was not there. They would have seen Dr. McLean and Dr. Carter and Gail Cooper from the bursar's office; they would not have seen her. It was silly, she told herself, to think they would have returned to Mayfield that night, but then Clive Lewis had come back and she would be mortified if they saw her in the café in the morning casually sipping tea. She would be embarrassed, humiliated. How would she be able to defend herself?

Clive remarked that they should find another seat; there were no windows near the table she had chosen, but he seemed to think better of saying more when Lila replied firmly, "This is where I want to sit."

He ordered tea for Lila and this time coffee for himself. "I need the caffeine," he said. "Long drive last night."

"Did you go because of Adriana?" Lila asked.

"I was there for personal reasons, yes. But I knew Ron. Well, not know him. I met him twice. Briefly. But I was also there for professional reasons."

"Professional reasons?" Suddenly Lila realized that she did not know what he did, how he made a living.

"I'm a lawyer," he said.

"You didn't tell me."

"You never asked."

He worked for a law firm in Mayfield, he said, which had another office in Brooklyn.

"Ah, Brooklyn. That's where you learned about Walcott."

"You win." He threw back his head and a dry laugh gurgled up his throat. "And, yes, I wouldn't have read him if one of the men in the Brooklyn office had not given me a copy of his book."

"Well, you read him. That's what matters," Lila said. A pause. Then, "So?"

He raised his eyebrows.

"You were going to tell me about the funeral."

He lifted his cup and exhaled. His breath upon the hot coffee raised steam over his face and changed the color of his eyes. They seemed gray to Lila, no longer blue. "Hundreds of people came," he said, half smiling, and yet she detected the undercurrent of melancholy in his voice. "The church was packed. Hundreds more outside. Many of them were holding Black Lives Matter posters. The police were there, of course. With their guns."

"Not drawn?"

"No. Not drawn, but ready to be drawn. Probably thirty, forty of them. Lots of police cars, a couple of ambulances. Like they were expecting trouble, but there was no trouble." He sipped his coffee. "The gospel choir was magnificent." His smile broadened on his lips. "Have you heard gospel music?"

Lila shook her head.

"You must. You won't hear it in Mayfield, but you should go to New York. To Harlem. You'll hear it there.

Those gospel singers reach down deep in their souls. When they sing, you find yourself reaching deep down in your own soul too."

"And how was the eulogy?"

"People cried when the pastor spoke. And there was not a dry eye in the church when Ron's brother gave the eulogy. I had to wipe away more than a couple of tears myself."

Lila was not oblivious to his pain, but she wanted to know. "Did you see Terrence or any of the others?" she asked softly, carefully.

"I saw Terrence. He was standing by my car when I left the church. He was waiting for me."

"You knew him too?"

"He and Ron were friends. Ron's family hired my firm to represent Ron. I agreed to work on the case."

Lila looked down on her hands. "There's so much I don't know."

Clive sat back in his chair and shaded his eyes. "I was young, just starting law school, when I read about what happened to Abner Louima." He dropped his hands from his face. They were trembling, but ever so slightly.

"Water?" Lila reached for the decanter on the table.

He shook his head. "It was because of Louima that I began taking cases in Brooklyn. He was from Haiti, poor, an immigrant." He ground his lower lip over his teeth, swallowed, and began again. It was still hard for him to talk about Louima, he said. What happened to the man was so disgusting he was ashamed to tell her.

"Tell me," Lila said. *Catharsis*. It was the relief tragedy offered.

So he told her how Louima was beaten by four policemen, how he was sexually assaulted, sodomized with a broken broomstick. How it took three surgeries to repair his colon and bladder.

How the four officers were exonerated.

Lila shut her eyes. "Then there was Amadou Diallo." Lila had been a student at university when Diallo was killed. Forty-one bullets, his body riddled with holes leaking blood. Like the other students in her class, she found comfort in convincing herself that such an atrocity could happen only in America. Not on her island.

"So you knew?"

"I felt terrible for Louima and Diallo . . ."

"Yes," he said flatly.

"It was horrible."

"I suppose to you it was an American problem, another case of police brutality in America," he said, uncannily echoing her thoughts. "But this is my country; I'm an American. I couldn't just stay on the sidelines. I had to do something. So I work on cases in Brooklyn. Sometimes."

He wasn't accusing her; she didn't think he was intimating that she should not have stood on the sidelines, a mere spectator, and yet she could not help feeling he disapproved of her response. Terrible, she had said. Horrible. She could have used those same words to describe any atrocity, but the atrocity he was speaking about was an American atrocity, his homeland's atrocity.

She could not match his anger, but she understood injustice. "They were white, weren't they, the policemen who tortured Louima and killed Diallo?" she offered.

"Ironic, isn't it?" He shrugged. "I didn't have to go

to Brooklyn. The same thing happened here in good old Mayfield. If Ron were white, they would have given him a chance. They would have seen there was nothing in his hands." He paused, and suddenly, as if an idea had just popped into his head, he leaned forward. Peering intensely into her eyes, he asked, "Did you see anything in his hands?"

Lila's heart dropped. She shifted her eyes. A second ticked away.

"How could you have seen?"

Another second ticked away. She kept her eyes averted from his.

He inhaled and his chest collapsed when he exhaled. "No, you couldn't have seen."

No, I couldn't have seen. The world had gone black and all she saw when light returned were his blue eyes.

"I found you keeled over on the pavement. Your head on your knees. How could you know?" He shook his head. "But if you had seen . . . if you had witnessed . . ."

Will he ask me? He's the lawyer Ron's family has hired. Will he ask me to be a witness against the police?

It's not your business, Robert said.

The moment passed. Clive leaned back in his seat. "I'm grabbing at straws," he said. "It was impossible. You couldn't have. You were bent over."

Yes, she was bent over. He had rescued her and her heartbeat returned to its regular rhythm. She faced him now. "You didn't see either."

"As I told you, it was all over when I arrived. I went back though."

Lila sighed. "After you helped me get to Mrs. Lowell's."

"I spoke to some people who were there."

"And will there be a trial?"

"For now, the police officers who shot Ron are on desk duty," he said.

"But after the trial?"

"It's virtually impossible to get a conviction for a police officer who unlawfully shot and killed someone, especially a Black man."

"So there won't be a trial?"

"We are going to make a case for a trial," he said.

"I saw some students protesting outside the cafeteria," she said, hoping to give him cause for optimism; he looked so despondent. "They had a banner with *Black Lives Matter* written on it."

"Some," he said dismissively.

"The students in my class on Thursday said not a word. It was as if Ron had not been killed. Then—"

"They are ashamed."

"Then yesterday a student, a female student, accused the town of being racist."

"It's systemic," Clive said. "It's in the air they breathe. Even I am not guilt free, but I try, I try really hard not to breathe in that stench. You live in America, you live in a town like Mayfield, and you are surrounded by lies, lies that try to convince you that white people are superior, that they are smarter, brighter, better looking than Black people. People hear that enough times, they see it enough times on TV, and they end up believing it. All lies. Lies." He stretched out his arm as if to reach for her hand. "But no one could say that about you, Lila. No one who has eyes."

She pulled her body away from him and dropped her hands on her lap.

"I know. I know. You're engaged. You have a fiancé. Robert."

"That's not the point," she said angrily. "I get so tired of these lame attempts to divide Black people under the guise of praising some of us. Whether they have eyes or not, no one can say that about Terrence either. Or about Elaine or Gail, or about the many, many Black people I know back home. White people are not smarter, brighter, better looking than Black people. Melanin—how much you don't have." She sucked in her breath. "The absence of melanin does not—"

"I know, Lila. I know. I didn't mean to suggest—"

"Then you should be more careful," she said.

"Lesson learned."

She waited until her heart had stopped pounding. "I know you didn't mean to say that I was an exception."

"Exceptional," he said.

She held up her hand. "Stop."

"They were wrong, you know, Lila, to leave without you," he said gently. "But they're not angry with you. You have to know that. They don't have anything against you. They just needed to be with each other."

"With their tribe," Robert said to her on the phone that night.

17

Back at her place, Lila clicked onto the Internet. She saw thousands. They flooded the streets for blocks near the church, chanting, "No justice, no peace," the young, the old, bearing posters denouncing police brutality against Black men, more than a few with placards about Ron's death. *Justice for Professor Brown. Prison for the killer cop.* Black Lives Matter signs were ubiquitous, mounted on tall wood poles, scrawled across brick walls, storefronts, even on sidewalks. Clive said he saw Terrence; he did not mention the others, but she saw them—Terrence, Elaine, and Gail—all the Black people at Mayfield, walking behind the front line of family mourners, Lila conspicuously missing.

Monday. The local newspaper in Mayfield carried a brief article, two paragraphs long, on the funeral. There were a few lines about the protest march in Brooklyn; many more lines reminding the people of Mayfield that in the American justice system one is presumed innocent until proven guilty. The police officers in question, who remained anonymous in the article, must be presumed innocent, the reporter wrote.

Terrence, Elaine, and Gail had returned to the campus. Lila went for lunch in the cafeteria knowing they would be there. They were cordial. They made room for her at their table.

Gail was the first one to speak: "We didn't think you'd want to come with us."

"You hadn't had a chance to know him," Terrence said, as if to validate Gail's explanation. He was methodically slicing his chicken, his eyes focused on his plate. His tone was nonjudgmental.

A fact. I did not know Ron Brown.

"Anyhow," Terrence said, raising his head and addressing Gail, "this isn't Lila's fight."

"Perhaps I should have gone," Lila murmured.

"We wouldn't have expected you to," Gail said.

She should say something now, Lila thought. She should offer her condolences. "I'm so sorry this happened."

"A man was killed," Terrence said. "That was the *this* that happened." His eyes met hers. She blinked and looked away.

Gail reached for her hand. "You haven't had your lunch, Lila. You better go now or there will be nothing good left to eat after the students take theirs."

Only once, as she stood in the food line waiting to be served, did Lila dare to look back at them. They were engaged in intense conversation. Elaine was leaning across the table, her shoulders strained forward, making a point that seemed to hold the full attention of the other two. Gail had her hands cupped around her chin. At one point, Terrence shook his head. They stopped talking when Lila returned to the table.

Elaine smiled at her. "Did you find something to eat?"

"I wasn't particularly hungry," Lila said. "I got the peas and rice."

"Peas and rice," Terrence sang out.

Peas and rice, quintessential Caribbean food. Was he mocking her?

"All the chicken was gone," Lila said.

He grinned. She tried again: "It wasn't right what those officers did to Ron."

Terrence smirked. "This whole thing is much bigger than Ron. It goes back centuries in this country. More than four hundred years."

"I heard that the officer who fired the bullet that killed Ron has been punished," she said.

"He still has his job, his pay with benefits." Terrence twisted his body in his seat and pulled his lips together, and for a second Lila thought he was going to spit on the ground. "The Mayfield police department will protect that man, that killer. All of Mayfield will. Racism is systemic; it filters through every aspect of our society. As well intentioned as they are, even liberals are affected."

Clive had said the same thing. No one is guilt free.

"That officer is no different from the people here," Terrence went on, his body still turned away from Lila. "He too was raised in a country where generations have vilified Black men. He has been conditioned, bred to assume that a Black man leaning over a white woman would not possibly be doing so out of kindness. He had to be assaulting her so he had to be stopped. That officer had the tacit permission of generations before him to shoot a Black man. He'll be exonerated. Just wait and see."

"Maybe not." Gail glanced at Lila, her eyes soft with empathy. "People are marching in the streets."

"Black people," Terrence returned.

"That's not fair," Gail said. "White people too."

"The Black people get beaten up and thrown in jail."

"The white people too."

Terrence snorted.

Elaine had remained quiet while Gail and Terrence exchanged barbs. Then abruptly her back shot up, ramrod straight. "That cop deserves the chair!" Her voice shook.

Lila could not tell whether Terrence and Gail agreed with Elaine. A few seconds passed and Gail stood up. A student was waiting for her in the bursar's office, she said. She didn't want to be late. It was not long before Terrence and Elaine followed her, Terrence apologizing to Lila for leaving her alone at the table to finish her lunch.

18

Lila could no longer put off the lecture she had promised she would give to the faculty. Dr. Campbell had proposed two dates, both to be scheduled before the next department meeting. Lila had chosen the later date, but it was coming up soon and she had to prepare her notes.

So much had changed, though. Clive's admission, Terrence's implied indictment—both still rang in her ears. And she had heard the voices bouncing off the walls of her office, faculty offering conflicting opinions.

"It was zealotry, of course," one of the professors pronounced. Lila recognized the voice; the speaker was an older man, gray-haired, stiff-lipped. "And that was understandable. It was definitely not pernicious intentions. You can't blame a police officer who has been trained to apprehend anyone—Black or white—he perceives to be in the act of committing a crime. The officer was almost certainly afraid for his life."

A younger voice broke through: "The officer was too impulsive, too quick to react. He should have moved closer to Ron. He would have seen that Ron was unarmed."

"How was the police officer to know Ron was unarmed?" another person offered. "He could have been killed if Ron had a gun."

A ripple of agreement.

"Ron was not that sort of man," the younger voice said. "He didn't carry a gun."

"But the officer couldn't know that."

"Well, Ron didn't have a gun and the cop would *not* have been killed if he had just taken the time to be sure. But he fired first and then checked afterward."

"Would you have been willing to take that chance to check first if you were the officer?"

More murmurings: *No. Not with my life. No.*

Then a whiny voice: "He disobeyed the order from the police."

And another: "Ron Brown always marched to the beat of his own drum. A stubborn man. Always objecting, even if you made a point that he agreed with. But that was his nature."

When Lila appeared to be within earshot, the arguments subsided. At those times, the faculty expressed their horror for what had happened to their colleague, sympathy for Ron's family, regret. Ron had such promise. *Such a nice guy. Just got his PhD.*

A professor from Ron's department approached her. "I think a memorial service on campus would be appropriate, don't you?"

His older colleague intervened: "Surely that would be *in*appropriate." He was one of the people Lila had overheard defending the police officers. *You can't blame them.* His voice was distinctive; it was a booming voice. "They are certain to have a memorial service for him in Brooklyn," he declared authoritatively. "That's where he came from, not so?"

Lila had no information to contribute. But others chimed in. Better people would give money to help defray the costs Ron's family would definitely be faced with rather than crowding the pews in a Brooklyn church with strangers who would be an imposition on the family's privacy.

So how to begin? Lila stared at the blank screen on her computer. They had whispered and tittered in the back of the room, chuckled slyly behind covered mouths when Dr. Campbell threw out her challenge. *Prove it*, Dr. Campbell seemed to say. *Prove that those Englishmen on the hill desired to appropriate Caliban, that vile savage.*

The room was small, a classroom, not a lecture room. She could see them all; there was no place for the coward to hide among the herd.

Dr. Campbell introduced her again. Oxford PhD. Seminal work. Her focus is on the errors Western critics have made in their interpretation of *The Tempest*. If the sarcasm in Dr. Campbell's tone had registered with the faculty, they did not to acknowledge it. To Lila, they presented blank faces.

Half an hour, the time she was given.

She began.

"It would be foolish to say those Englishmen on the hill wanted to be like Caliban, to imitate him."

Lila glanced at Dr. Campbell in the front row, scribbling on a notepad. She had yielded her place behind her desk to Lila, but Lila had chosen to stand.

"That is, Caliban as he is interpreted by the West," Lila clarified. "It would be ridiculous to claim that those Englishmen would want to be like him, an unredeemable savage whose 'vile race' 'had that in't which good natures / Could not abide to be with.'"

Some heads turned downward.

"That is not my point at all," she said. Reading Baldwin had helped her clarify her position. "It is Caliban's speech I am referring to, those lines so often recited, as if that savage . . ." She paused for the effect she wanted. She knew they were uncomfortable. Let them be, she said to herself. Let them think of the character they reviled. "And yet," she continued, "Shakespeare gave Caliban the most beautiful, the most lyrical lines in the play. *Be not afeared.*

"What were those sailors afraid of, the ones who had been shipwrecked on Caliban's island? Of birds singing to each other? Of feathers fluttering in the trees? Leaves swaying in the breeze? A branch breaking, twigs crunching under the feet of animals? The beat of raindrops on the matted earth? 'The isle is full of noises, / Sounds, and sweet airs, that give delight, and hurt not.'"

Dr. Campbell crossed her arms, frowned.

"No," Lila said. "To the sailors those sounds were not sweet; they did not give delight. They did not hear them the way Caliban did. And why? Because they saw Caliban's world through *their* eyes, not through Caliban's eyes."

No reaction from Dr. Campbell. Some faculty sat forward; they seemed interested.

Lila then went on to talk about the work of Roberto Fernández Retamar, the Cuban literary critic. For Retamar, Caliban was a revolutionary. She pointed to *The Pleasures of Exile* by George Lamming, the Barbadian novelist. He, too, had defended Caliban and so had Aimé Césaire, the playwright from Martinique, in his play *La Tempête*. "They had seen Caliban's world through Caliban's eyes. Through his point of view."

Someone coughed. It sounded authentic, not an attempt to express displeasure or objection to what she had said.

Her quarrel, Lila explained, was with the appropriation of Caliban's words by people who condemned him. "People loved Caliban's words, but they rejected *him*, Caliban, the person, the human being."

"Hip-hop." A voice from the back row. A student, young, pale-faced, light-brown hair falling to his shoulders. The president of the English Club. Dr. Campbell said he would be there. "My generation loves hip-hop. We play it all the time," he said. "We dance to it."

Her point exactly. "But do they empathize with the people whose stories we hear about in the lyrics of hip-hop? The tales of oppression, economic hardship, neglect?" She wanted to add *police brutality*, but thought the better of it. Too soon. After the inquest perhaps.

Light applause. Dr. Campbell nodded. Reluctantly, Lila thought.

19

She stood outside Terrence's office. Terrence had told her he had waited for her to come to Mayfield—*they* had waited for her—because of what she had written in her essay. She wanted to explain. Before he could hear about her lecture from the faculty in her department, she wanted him to know she had not recanted. She had read Baldwin. Those Englishmen had the same rights to Caliban's lyrical lines as she had, as all human beings had. His words were part of the human heritage. But she had not changed her fundamental position: the British had committed crimes against humanity. They had seized her island, dragged Africans in chains across the Atlantic to plant sugarcane for them. They had built their mansions on the backs of Black people.

Terrence was walking down the corridor when she spotted him. Two male students flanked him, one of them speaking to him passionately, his hands punching the air. She recognized the young man. She could see the tattoo of a flower, its stem curling up his neck. Terrence noticed her and stopped, raised his hand in greeting, and pointed to the students. He said something to them and they glanced at her and back to him. They didn't seem happy when he put his hand firmly on the shoulder of the student who was doing the most talking. They both turned and headed in the opposite direction and Terrence walked briskly toward her.

"I didn't expect a visit from you," he said, unlocking his office door to let her in.

"I hope I didn't interrupt your conversation with your students."

He laughed. "Conversation? That's an odd way to describe it. Do you have *conversations* with your students?"

"Sometimes," she said, following him into his office. Her eyes swept across the room. Pictures of Malcolm X, Martin Luther King Jr., and some Black men and women she did not know were mounted on the wall. There were books everywhere, some of them on the ground, apparently having fallen off the tightly packed bookcase which was sagging slightly to one side.

"You chat with them?" Terrence asked, picking up the volumes from the floor and stacking them next to an untidy pile that cluttered his desk. "Have a heart-to-heart with them?"

"I listen to them," she said.

He straightened up. "Well, that's what I was doing."

She felt foolish. The students were the ones talking; he had been nodding his head. Had she unconsciously tried to belittle his interactions with his students, impugn his professionalism? She was mortified that such a motive could have been behind her choice of word. *Conversation.* Clearly he was not having a conversation with the students, idly gossiping.

She was aware he had been watching her as she scanned his office. It was half the size of hers. There was barely enough space for his desk, two chairs, and the bookcase, but there was a window. She walked toward it. "You get a great view of the mountain from here," she said.

"I could have asked for a bigger office," he said, "but I liked seeing that mountain. It reminds me that there's a god."

Her eyebrows shot up.

"Surprised? Did you think I was a heathen? An atheist? Most Black Americans believe in God, you know. We are probably the most religious people in America. You can barely walk two blocks in a Black neighborhood before you run into a church. You must have heard the Negro spirituals."

"'Amazing Grace,'" she said.

"Well, we didn't write that one. If you go to the Library of Congress, you'll see this inscription: *Words, John Newton; melody, unknown*. But we know where the melody came from. It came from the bowels of the slave ship, from the groans, the cries, the prayers of enslaved Africans. From the clanking of the iron chains around their legs. Hear. Listen."

She waited as he beat out the sorrowful rhythm with his foot. *Dum, thump; dum, thump; dum, thump; dum, thump*, the thumps hard and ferocious against the thinly carpeted floor.

"John Newton was a captain of a slave ship," he said, stilling his foot. "That's where he heard that painful melody. He had a conversion, but before that, he bought and sold human beings, trafficked them on a slave ship that stacked Africans attached to each other like floorboards, heads to feet, feet to heads, in the hold of the ship, and then dragged them, chained by their necks and ankles, to my part of the world." He searched her face as if expecting a response from her. When she said nothing, he added, "Dragged them to your world too."

"I see Martin Luther King Jr.," she said.

"Everybody knows Martin Luther King Jr.," he said gruffly. He stretched his top lip stiffly over his teeth and shook his head. She winced.

"And Malcom X," she said quickly, feeling the sting of his scorn. "You have an excellent photograph of him."

His face relaxed. "King has a national holiday, but without Malcolm X, I think it would have been harder for him to get the people behind him. I'm talking about the grassroots who marched through the streets."

"His mother was from Grenada. From *my* part of the world."

He frowned at her momentarily, and then swiped his hand across his mouth and said, "I didn't mean to imply—"

"Oh, you said enough to me in the cafeteria."

"Is that why you're here?"

"Where I come from we were the seasoning place where they tried to break the Africans. Ready them for the plantations," she said. *That's why I'm here. To remind you that Africans were enslaved in the Caribbean.*

"Sit, sit." He pointed to the chair facing his desk. "I shouldn't have talked like that. Saying it's not your fight. I know racism doesn't only happen in America. What I meant was . . ." He sat down and shoved away the pile of papers in front of him. "But this is our country, Lila, and we have to solve our problems. African Americans have to take the lead."

There was an intensity in his voice that compelled her to make an admission she had not planned: "I saw when that policeman shot Ron."

In an instant his face darkened and rows of thin wavelets crossed his forehead. He pressed his hands on his desk and bent toward her, his shoulders raised, the muscles on his neck strained. "Did you tell this to anyone?"

"I told Robert."

"Robert?"

"My fiancé," she said. "Back home."

"So are you going to report what you saw?"

"I'm not sure if it would help," she said. "They—the police—may not put too much worth in what I have to say."

"And why is that?"

"I'm here only as a visitor. And . . ."

"And what, Lila?"

"And I can't be sure."

"Of what you saw?"

Her fingers twitched nervously. If she reported what she believed she saw, she would have to go to court as a witness. She would need a lawyer. She did not have money for that.

And what would be the worth of her word against the word of an American officer of the law? She was here at the pleasure and goodwill of the US government. It was the US government that had granted Mayfield College permission to hire her. Her work permit could be yanked. She could be sent back home.

She knew Terrence was waiting for her answer. She looked down on her hands. She could not bear the glare from his eyes.

"But you did see, right?" His eyes were still fixed on her. "You said you saw."

"I said I saw *when* it happened. I cannot be sure that I saw *what* happened."

Terrence threw back his head and laughed; it was a laugh without humor, a sad, accusatory laugh. "A fine distinction, but a distinction all right between *when* and *what*. But I don't blame you, Lila. Like I said, this is not your problem. You can go back to your sunny island. We live here. We have to face the racism here."

"I wanted you to know," she said softly.

"To know what?"

"That Ron was innocent."

He laughed again. "My dear West Indian girl, you do not have to tell us that. We know; we have decades, hundreds of years of knowing. The police are always right; Black men like Ron are always wrong, always guilty in their eyes." He began gathering his books and papers on his desk. "I have to go. Those students . . ." He pointed to the door. "I told them I'd meet them in the library."

He was dismissing her! But his condescension had irked her too. *My dear West Indian girl.*

He let her leave first, standing back politely at his office door to let her pass through, and then he walked away, in the opposite direction.

He was angry with her. She could hear his footsteps clacking nosily down the hallway. And perhaps she had given him reason to be condescending. She was a coward; she had squirmed her way out of taking a stand with her simpering *when* and *what*. Yet she had a legitimate excuse, sensible reasons for not committing herself to any statement that would implicate her as a witness, that would invalidate the police officer's claim, accuse him of lying. This was not her country; she could be deported.

What's Hecuba to him, or he to Hecuba / That he should weep for her? The lines drifted through her head, Hamlet paralyzed by inaction, in awe of an actor who is moved to tears by the death of someone the actor could never have known.

She felt ashamed. Clive had become a lawyer because of the brutalization of Louima and the forty-one bullets pumped into Amadou Diallo two years later. Abner Louima was not an American; Amadou Diallo was not an American, not by birth. Both immigrants and yet, Clive, an American, had fought for them. His conscience would not allow him to stand still and do nothing while Black men became targets for corrupt police officers.

She remembered the awe she felt when there, on television, for the whole world to witness, was the former mayor of New York City, David Dinkins, in front of the police headquarters surrounded by angry protesters, his arms drawn behind his back, handcuffed. He would not stand still either when the police officers who shot Diallo walked free in the streets of New York.

No person on her island who had held such a high office as David Dinkins once held would ever have exposed himself to such public disgrace, handcuffed like a common criminal. No one in his position would have voluntarily taken the risk that he could be arrested and thrown in jail.

My dear West Indian girl.

Terrence spoke of *us* and *we*. Dinkins was African American; he was part of *us* and *we*. He belonged to the people who had decades, hundreds of years of knowing. Amadou Diallo's people were not from America; they were from Guinea, Africa. Yet Dinkins would risk his reputation for such a man, risk his standing among powerful men in black tails and white bow ties who had opened their pocketbooks for him, bankrolled his campaign for mayor.

What if the shoe were on the other foot? Would people from her island come out in the public square to protest the unjustified killing of an innocent man by the police if that man were an immigrant to their island? Lila did not know the answer.

20

She saw the edge of a white envelope sticking out from the slit at the bottom of her office door. She picked it up. It was sealed, no name on the outside. Perhaps a note from George Tilling, one of her students, asking for an extension for a paper that was due a week ago. He had requested an extension for another paper in the same way, with an unmarked envelope slipped under her door. She had long suspected that he was finding it difficult to keep up with the rest of the class. He never asked a question and when she sought his opinion on a point another student had made, he usually shook head and lowered his eyes to his desk. She did not force him to answer her, noticing too that the other students didn't seem to mind that he never contributed to the discussion. She had had students like George Tilling before. They were either shy or afraid to speak for fear of exposing their inability to grasp the material. She suspected that George Tilling fell into the latter category. She would talk to him, she decided, recommend he get help from a tutor or perhaps request early withdrawal from the class so that his GPA would not be affected. She set the envelope down on her desk. She would read his note later.

She was taking out her papers from her briefcase when she became conscious of a faint scent of perfume that she had dismissed when she opened her office door. Now, simply wanting to confirm that her imagination was not playing tricks on her, she began sniffing the air around her. Perhaps she had sprayed too much perfume on her wrists, but what she had smelled was not the perfume she used. She sniffed her briefcase, inside and outside. Nothing. The briefcase smelled of old leather, the papers inside odorless. She walked back to her office door. The scent was there, but barely. She returned to her desk. The scent was stronger now. *It had to be the envelope!* She reached for her letter opener and slit the top of the envelope. A blast of a musky odor, so strong, so pungent, sent a shiver down her back. Inside was a piece of paper, folded in three parts. She unfolded it.

PUPPET OF THE COLONIZER. READ FANON.

The words were in caps, in black ink. There was no signature, no identifying marks. Except the scent.

The note would not be from George Tilling; the scent on it would not have come from Mayfield, Vermont. A damp sweat broke out on her forehead. She could identify it! Not by name. By its type. It was the scent of oils sold in the street markets on her island. The vendors who sold it wore African garb.

21

Her first instinct was to tell no one, not even Robert. He would urge her to come home; she did not belong in that place, he would say again. No, she could not tell Robert.

Terrence! He had not accused her directly, but he had insinuated, with his swipe at her, that she belonged to a past era, a time when the British named her chain of islands. *My dear West Indian girl*, Terrence had said. But the colonizers already knew that Columbus had made a mistake, thinking he was en route to India.

Colonized intellectuals. It was a term Frantz Fanon used for the middle class from former colonized countries like her own. People like her family. People so brainwashed by the colonizer that their highest aspirations were to be like the colonizers, to imitate them in every way, in manners, in values, in language.

Speak like the English. Speak like the French.

Before Patrick Chamoiseau, Fanon had argued for nation language. He was chastised as a child for speaking the Creole French of his native island Martinique. He was admonished to speak French-French. Later, at university, his studies in medicine and psychiatry would open his eyes to the insidious effects on one's sense of identity, one's sense of pride in one's humanity, when one rejected one's language for the language of the colonizer. He would write about the danger to one's self-esteem in the implicit acceptance of the superiority of the colonizer.

PUPPET OF THE COLONIZER. READ FANON. Terrence would have read Fanon. *The Wretched of the Earth*: he would have read that book and *Black Skin, White Masks* too.

But had she not defended Fanon's warnings to the middle class? When her students declared that Tee, the main character in Hodge's novel, spoke a dialect, a patois, hadn't she insisted that the language Tee spoke was a legitimate language, as legitimate as what they spoke in Mayfield? It was nation language, she said. *Their* language.

Terrence was asking for her loyalty when he pressed her to report what she saw, to tell the police she was there when Ron was gunned down. She had fumbled, wavered, dithered, equivocated, defending herself with the absurd distinction between *when* and *what*. Terrence had laughed at her. Even now she could hear the echoes of his scorn.

Yet still, it seemed implausible to her that Terrence would have stooped so low as to put an anonymous note under her door. He was a proud man. He would have confronted her directly. He would have accused her face-to-face of being a puppet of the colonizer.

Then she remembered the student with the dark ponytail who had stood with the others at the entrance of the cafeteria, next to the Black Lives Matter banner. He was the same one who had told her about the funeral. She recognized him again when she was waiting for Terrence outside his office door. She did not mistake the look of resentment he threw toward her when Terrence saw her and waved.

It would be that student who had put that note under her door, but it would have been Terrence who had filled his head with arguments he could use against her.

She would show Clive Lewis the note. Clive was a lawyer; he could help her, protect her.

Her head swirled. How could she trust Clive Lewis? He had dissimulated, if not directly, then indirectly, giving her a pass when she was certain he believed she had seen the police shoot Ron Brown.

They did not trust her. Neither of them.

Clive was working with Terrence. Didn't he say they spoke at the funeral, that Terrence knew that Ron's family had hired his law firm to represent Ron?

They were playing good cop/bad cop. Terrence would confront her directly; Clive would avoid the question completely. Yet they both wanted the same thing. They wanted her to be a witness against the officer who had shot Ron. If Terrence had instigated a student to send her that message, Clive would know too. It would be foolish to think he would protect her.

22

Lila had another sleepless night. She tossed and turned in her bed, tormented by the accusation in the note. She had quoted Fanon to acquaintances of her grandmother who spoke of the glory days when the British ruled their island. In those glory days, there was no crime, no drugs, they claimed. People respected their superiors, gave deference to the ones on the high rung of the ladder. We had a civil society then, they said, held together by norms of acceptable behavior, codes of good manners that all respected, the rich, the poor.

Know your place! How many times had she heard those words, even from well-intentioned people? How she had railed against those who thought this way! How she had tried to get them to understand the psychology of colonialism! A small island like England can rule most of the world, their island too, because the English had *trained* the people they had colonized to do the work for them. They had brainwashed them, convinced them of the superiority of British culture, British beauty, British intellect.

Her island had made inroads since it had achieved political independence from England. No longer was all the literature schoolchildren were made to read literature by English writers, no longer was the history they were taught British history, the perspective on the world presented through a British lens. The curriculum had changed; the books had changed, but the annual Carnival celebration told the story of how much had remained the same. There, on the main Grand Stand where the costumers paraded, class and color were exposed for everyone to see: the bands grouped (or chose to be grouped) by color, people with light skin with people with light skin; people with dark skin with people with dark skin.

The British had left; few who remained were pure white. Too many overseers, too many slave owners, had spread their seed across the plantations, taking the African women they had enslaved for their pleasure. But the legacy of the British was deeply ingrained; the caste system of color and money still vibrantly alive.

She had fought against any association with that kind of neocolonial thinking. And here she was: the accusation in her hand.

She needed to speak to someone she could trust, someone who could advise her on what she should do. Gail had seemed remorseful. Even if she had not quite admitted that she and her friends had deliberately left her behind when they went to Ron's funeral, abandoning her as if she were some alien outcast (a spy?), Gail seemed to have sympathy for her.

Gail would be an impartial judge. Hadn't she reprimanded Terrence? White people protested too; they marched in the streets, she told him.

They met at the small park at the edge of the town, near the lake. Lila pulled out the note from the plastic bag she had zippered up tightly. Gail's reaction was immediate. She wrinkled her nose and thrust the envelope away from her. "Wow! Where did you get this, Lila? The scent is strong."

"Open it," Lila said. "You'll see how much stronger."

"Musk oil," Gail said, bringing the envelope close to her nose. "What's this about?"

"Open it," Lila said again. "I didn't reseal it."

Gail lifted the flap. "Jesus! It *is* strong."

"Read the note."

"PUPPET OF THE COLONIZER. READ FANON. Nothing else. No signature. Where did you get this, Lila?"

"Someone slipped it under my office door."

Gail sniffed the envelope again. "It's not the real Egyptian musk oil; it's fake." She brought the envelope even closer to her nose. "But a good imitation of the original. This one was probably made with a plant base. Ambrette seed. They call it musk mallow."

"At first I thought it was a student who put it under my door," Lila said.

"No. It's too expensive. The students here have better things to do with their money. Perfume would not be one of them."

"Then I thought that even if it *was* a student who had put that note under my door, he had help."

"Help? From who?"

"Terrence," Lila said.

Gail shook her head. "You are wrong, Lila. Terrence is angry. He wants justice for his friend. He's grieving. But this is not like Terrence. He wouldn't do something like that."

"You heard what he said at lunch."

"He didn't mean it."

"*Peas and rice*, he said. I didn't miss how he said it. He was taunting me. His intention was to exclude me from all of you. Now he's explicit. *Puppet of the colonizer*. That's more than explicit."

"Terrence wouldn't do this," Gail said again, and returned the note to the envelope. "Here. Take it."

Lila slipped the envelope into the plastic bag. "And yet I wonder how a student from here, from Mayfield in Vermont, would know about African oils," she said, spacing out her words slowly.

"What are you saying, Lila?"

"I'm saying that Terrence could have given it to one of his students. Not the oil. The paper perfumed with the oil."

"But why? Why would he do that?"

So Lila told Gail of her meeting with Terrence. "He wants me to speak to the police. I was there. Elaine too, but she was on the other side of the street."

"So you saw?"

"I heard the shots."

"But you saw?"

Lila turned away.

Gail moved closer to her. "You told me what Terrence wants you to do, but what do *you* want to do, Lila?"

"I don't know."

"You don't know?"

Lila clasped her hand to her mouth and sucked in her breath through her nose. She exhaled and said, her voice breathy, "You read what was on that note. Terrence thinks I'm—"

"An Uncle Tom?" Gail finished the words for her.

"Puppet of the colonizer. Uncle Tom. They mean the same. It was a coward who sent this to you. He didn't even have the courage to give his name. Terrence would never send someone an anonymous note."

"A student he encouraged would," Lila said.

"When a student sets their mind to do something, they don't need encouragement. Especially not from a professor."

"What about the scent on the paper?" Lila said.

"A student could have gotten it from any professor's office."

"*African* oil?"

"Well, if it was a student, they wouldn't have gotten it from me," Gail said emphatically. "I'd tear up that note if I were you. The envelope too."

Lila sealed the plastic bag.

"You're going to keep it?" Gail stared at her.

Lila didn't answer her.

Gail ran her hand across her forehead and wiped away the beads of sweat that had pearled there. "Let's sit," she said. "I can't keep standing. There's a bench over there."

"We can leave," Lila said quickly.

"Come." Gail was already walking toward the bench. "Here." She stopped and eased her ample body down. "Sit next to me. I want to know your plans. What are you going to do with that note?"

Lila sat down next to Gail and put the plastic bag in her briefcase.

"I see," Gail said, following Lila's movements. "Well, you take care of yourself. But I want to know about Ron. What are you going to do about Ron?"

"I'm not a puppet . . ." Lila wrapped her fingers tightly around the handles of her briefcase and held it firmly on her lap.

"I know, I know." Gail patted Lila's knee sympathetically. "I wasn't saying—"

"Ron was innocent," Lila said.

"Then why won't you say so, report what you saw to the police?" Gail removed her hand from Lila's knee.

"I'm not from this country. I'm not a citizen."

"Are you afraid you'll get in trouble?"

"It's possible. I'm a guest of the college. I don't want to make trouble for them."

"And how would you do that?"

"I don't want to have the college's name splashed across the newspapers because of me."

"It's too late for that," Gail said. "The college's name is already in the papers. Ron taught here. Terrence teaches here."

"And Terrence belongs here." Lila looked across the park toward the lake and pulled her cardigan tightly across her chest. She would have to add layers under her sweater when she got back to Mrs. Lowell's.

"They are accusing Ron of being a drug dealer," Gail said softly. "Adriana's supplier."

Lila turned away from the lake. "Adriana was in love with him," she said.

"How did you know?"

"Clive Lewis told me."

"He's the lawyer Ron's family hired." Gail stated the fact as if she expected Lila would know it too.

"He said Ron split up with Adriana and she was heartbroken."

Gail sighed. "I think Adriana was waiting for Ron at the restaurant."

"So you all knew?"

"It was supposed to be a secret," Gail said, "but Elaine found out. She and Ron argued about it."

"About the affair?"

"All I know is that after their argument, Ron broke up with Adriana."

"Terrence disapproved too," Lila said.

"Not in the same way. It was personal with Elaine."

It's personal with some of the women on my island too. They feel rejected by Black men who choose white women. "And was it political with Terrence?"

"You could say so."

"And now I must do the politically right thing. Is that it?" Lila said.

"The *morally* right thing."

"And if I say Ron was trying to save Adriana, that his mouth was on hers because he was trying to breathe life into her, will the police believe me?"

"You'll have to tell them what you saw." Gail stood up. "I have to go back to the office. My advice to you: destroy the note. Do the right thing and you won't have to worry about the idiot who wrote that foolish note."

The right thing. Lila sucked in the cool air; mist formed when she exhaled.

23

She saw him the next day, the student she believed had put the note under her door. She was walking down the front steps of the academic building and there he was, not far away, sitting on a bench with a group of students. Someone had made a joke and they burst out laughing. Maybe it was a reflex, the toss of his head when he laughed, that made him turn sideways, and when he did, she saw that he had noticed her too. He turned back, stood up, said something to his friends, and began walking quickly down the pathway.

He's trying to avoid me! She wanted to call out to him but she didn't know his name. What would she say, "Hey, you, stop!"? And she couldn't run after him. A Black woman pursuing a young white man? People might call the police.

She followed him, walking fast, though not so fast as to attract attention. She could see him ahead of her but she lost sight of him at the bend in the pathway where there was a cluster of tall pine trees. By then she was out of breath, weighed down by her briefcase in one hand, a pile of student papers in the other, her feet aching from the pressure of her high heels on the hard surface of the pathway. She slowed down and was about to give up when he jumped out of the bushes. Her heart leapt in her throat. Did he mean to harm her? But he approached her with a wide smile across his lips. "Professor," he said calmly, "I heard you behind me."

He was wearing a long black coat that fell midcalf and under it a black sweatshirt, the hood drawn over his head, black jeans cut off above his ankles so that one could not miss his black leather boots with the double row of silver buckles on the straps glinting menacingly. *Menacingly? A silly thought.* They were attractive boot buckles; on any other occasion she would have admired them.

"Were you trying to reach me?" He raised his chin, a pretentious pose, though it nevertheless gave him an air of sincerity.

"Trying to reach you? Oh, not at all," she said haltingly. "What made you think so?"

"You were walking fast. I thought to catch up with me."

"I wasn't walking fast just now," she said.

He extended his hand and she shook it. "I'm Steve. Steve Hunter," he said. "Perhaps you couldn't see me. The bushes . . ."

"We've spoken before," she said.

He wrinkled his brow.

"You were the student who told me that the coroner had released Professor Brown's body. And I saw you again in the hallway. Outside of Professor Carter's office."

"Yes. I remember now."

"He's your professor?"

"And friend," he said.

"I should apologize for interrupting you. You seemed to be in the midst of an intense discussion with Professor Carter. I didn't mean to take you away from him."

Steve shrugged. "I caught up with Professor Carter. I met with him later. No harm done."

But *was* there harm done? How does she say to him: *I know you stuck that note under my door. I know Professor Carter put you up to it.* She had no grounds to accuse him. The note was typed. There would be no way, even if she could get hold of something he had written, to identify him. She would have to find another way to trap him into admitting the note was his. Then an idea occurred to her.

"Professor Carter is quite a scholar of Fanon," she said, keeping her voice even. "I suppose he must have told you how much Fanon's work has affected people in my part of the world."

He flinched, or she thought he did. He sucked in his breath and his hands twitched, but this happened in the blink of an eye. Before she could be certain, he was casually removing the hood from his head. His long brown hair tumbled to his shoulders. He pulled an elastic band from his wrist and tied it back. Lila could see the black tattoo of a leafy vine with a flower at the top.

"Fanon?" There was a half smile on his lips, a mocking smile, it seemed to Lila. "Professor Carter never spoke to me about Fanon."

"*Black Skin, White Masks?*"

He shrugged. "A book by this Fanon?"

"Frantz Fanon," she said. "He also wrote *The Wretched of the Earth.*"

Steve swiped his hand down his ponytail. "Never heard of it. Or that other book either."

"Professor Carter never mentioned Fanon to you?"

"Never mentioned. Not those books." Students were passing by them. He twisted his head in the direction of one of them. "Later," he said, and raised his hand.

Then, with the insouciance of someone who had not the slightest reason to be worried about Lila's pointed inquiries, he turned back and said, "Going to the library, Professor?"

Lila glanced down at the papers in her hand. "I have a lot to read. Student essays."

"If I was going your way," he said, "I'd walk with you, but I just remembered I left a book in my class."

He was walking fast again when he left her, headed in the opposite direction, toward the academic building with the faculty offices. He would tell Terrence of their meeting, she had no doubt.

Lila could not blame him. It takes twenty-five years for young people to begin to understand their own minds, to have confidence in their own thoughts. Gail was wrong; in the hands of a charismatic, persuasive professor, a young person could be easily manipulated.

A harsh word, *manipulate*, and yet Lila was convinced that was what Terrence had done. She did not believe he had instructed Steve to put that note under her door. Neither did she believe he had typed the words. It was possible too that he had not known what Steve had done, but the more she thought about it, the more it seemed to her that Terrence was responsible for inflaming Steve against her.

She knew firsthand the power professors could wield over students, especially students on the verge of adulthood, nervous about the future that looms before them and hungry for guidance, for the paths they should take, the ones they should avoid.

She was young herself, not much older than her students, in her first year teaching college students, spouting opinions as if they were facts, when she learned the tragic consequence of believing in her absolute authority in the classroom. There was a young Indian girl in her class, seventeen, possibly eighteen. Her parents had arranged for her to marry the son of a wealthy man. The girl had no objections. Arranged marriages were traditional in her culture. Besides, her family was poor. The marriage would be a coup for them.

"But do you love him?" Lila, the novice professor, had asked.

"I like him."

"But love him?"

The girl had shrugged.

"You should marry the man you love," Lila told the girl, and gave her Jane Austen's most romantic novels, *Pride and Prejudice* and *Sense and Sensibility*. The girl read them and afterward she broke her engagement.

Weeks later, Lila found her student weeping over her books in the library. Her parents were devastated; the marriage was their hope of lifting their daughters out of poverty. For there was a second daughter who could have also benefited from the association with rich in-laws.

"I could have learned to love him," the girl said.

In the end, Lila was relieved to discover that the man was actually in love with the young girl and gave her a second chance.

Had Lila too been bound by tradition when she acquiesced to her grandmother's plea to give herself time to think of the consequences of marrying a divorced man? No one in her family had broken that strict Catholic rule. The invitation from Mayfield was a convenient excuse, but she had wondered if Robert was right to ask if she truly loved him. For if she truly loved Robert, would it have mattered that her grandmother objected?

She would not make the same mistake again of imposing her opinions on her students. She would teach, she would listen, she would ask questions. She would prompt her students to think for themselves.

Had Terrence done that? Had he encouraged the young Steve to form his own judgments, to assess the validity of what had been told to him? Or had he given him Fanon—*Black Skin, White Masks*; *The Wretched of the Earth*—and filled Steve's head with righteous indignation against the people who had cooperated with the colonists in the French colonies of Algeria, Martinique, Guadeloupe?

Had Terrence told young Steve that Lila was a witness to the injustice inflicted on a Black man by a white man? Lila could imagine Steve hearing this, eyes blazing, choking with righteous anger. *We got that lying cop now! We have a witness. He won't stand a chance. He'll go to prison for life.*

And then Terrence would tell him Lila was juggling *what* and *when*.

24

I t had been more than a week since she had spoken to Robert. He had called her twice; each time she had not taken the call. The second time she could sense his anxiety in the message he left. She had to reassure him of her love for him, her intention to marry him.

The note under her door had rattled her. She had been reluctant to call Robert but now she needed to have her confidence restored.

"Gothic," Robert said. "It's the style."

All she had told him at that point was that there was a young man in black—black coat, black sweatshirt, shiny silver buckles on his boots—who had tried to run away from her. She had described the tattoo on his neck. He'd frightened her, she said.

"I don't think that young man's clothes have anything to do with some malevolent intentions," Robert said. "If you're thinking he was wearing black because he belongs to one of those violent gangs, you're wrong. Anyhow, didn't you say it was a tattoo of a flower on his neck? I would think you would have had reason to suspect him if it was a tattoo of a skull or something like that, something macabre or violent. A flower to me suggests love, peace. It's what young people do to rebel against old folks like us. They dress up in black and put tattoos on their bodies."

Lila disguised her embarrassment with a light retort: "We are still young."

"When we were young, as young as your young man, our parents didn't like our style either," Robert said.

She laughed. "I remember when I wore my hair so short you could see my scalp."

"It's good to hear you laugh, Lila. I was beginning to worry that you were getting yourself caught up in all that stuff."

Something shifted in Lila's chest and choked back the laughter. She found herself saying, "I told him."

"Told who?" Robert too had stopped laughing.

"Terrence."

It seemed like an eternity before Robert spoke again. "And what did you promise him, Lila?"

"Nothing. I told him I couldn't be sure of what I saw."

"Good, good."

"Then I got this note slipped under my door."

"A note?"

"It said, *Puppet of the colonizer. Read Fanon.*"

Robert grunted, a guttural sound that scratched against his vocal cords. "Oh, Lila. I warned you . . ."

"I think the student who ran from me did it."

"It said *puppet.* I warned you, Lila."

"There was some kind of perfumed oil on the paper."

"Perfumed oil?"

"It smelled like one of those African oils they sell at our African market."

"Where would a student from Vermont get African oil? Please make sense."

"I think Terrence put that student up to it."

"What have you got yourself into, Lila?"

"He could have got it from Terrence's office."

"And what, Lila? A student found some oil in Terrence's office and stole it? Is that what you're saying?"

"No. He got the *paper* from Terrence's office."

"And somehow the oil got on the paper?"

"The scent of those oils is strong. You know that, Robert. Sometimes all it takes is for someone to brush against you and for the rest of the day you can smell the oil on your body?"

"I want you to think through what you are saying. The scent of the oil in Terrence's office was so strong that even a blank piece of paper on his desk would smell of it?"

Her theory was beginning to unravel. What Robert was saying made sense. She had been in Terrence's office; she had sat close to him. If the oil had come from Terrence, his office would have been suffused with its scent.

"For that matter, it could have been anyone in your department," said Robert. "Someone who doesn't want you there."

Who could hate her so much that they would want to defame her character? She had been aware of the faculty's discontent with the changes in the curriculum, the dwindling literature program in the English Department. More Comp 1 and 2, fewer courses in the Great Books, in the works of the master writers the faculty had studied in graduate school. The faculty were disgruntled, frustrated.

They had welcomed her to Mayfield, but Lila knew she was a threat. It would be impossible after her, after the course she was teaching, to go back to the way things were. Every seat in her class was taken. Already registration had started for the next semester and enrollment in her class had almost reached its maximum.

Lila was pleased yet she was not so arrogant as to believe she was the reason for the popularity of her course, that it was her teaching style that had drawn more students to sign up for it in the spring semester. They had enrolled in her course in Caribbean literature before they met her. Before she had arrived at Mayfield, students were already demanding courses that were relevant to the world they lived in. Technology had shrunk the distances between cultures and countries; it had made the rest of the world more reachable. If they were to succeed in the increasing pace of technology, the students knew they had to learn about people across the globe with whom it was most likely they would have to interact.

Was there someone in the English Department so insecure that he or she would cook up a plan to force her to leave, someone who would try to intimidate her, frustrate her, attack her character, make her life so unpleasant that she would want to return home?

"Leave that place, Lila," Robert said. "Come back home."

"Christmas," she said. "I promise I'll be home for Christmas."

"Then promise me you won't say anything more about what you saw, or *thought* you saw when that professor was shot. I know you want to get along with everyone, but now you have people putting nasty notes under your door. Puppet of the colonizer? You are anything but, Lila. You know that, I know that. And you have no idea who'd want to say something so libelous about you. Was it a student? Was it Terrence? Was it some jealous professor in your department? You don't know."

"Christmas," she repeated.

"And you plan to return afterward?"

"My contract is for the entire academic year," she said. "Until June."

Robert sighed. "And then we will get married?"

"And then we will get married."

25

It was late October and the dean of the School of Liberal Arts had decided to give a reception for the faculty. A sort of pre-Thanksgiving celebration, he said. Robert scoffed when Lila told him about the invitation. They are celebrating the bamboozling of the Native Americans, he said. But Robert's family import/export business thrived in the months leading up to Thanksgiving, for Thanksgiving had become a popular American import to their island, to all of the Caribbean in fact: turkey, stuffing, canned yellow American sweet potatoes, canned cranberry sauce, canned chestnuts, all the trimmings. Robert, however, also set his sights on selling back to America, having America import Caribbean goods, his goods. "We target the organic food market," he told Lila. "Chataigne tastes just like chestnuts. And America's health foodies love our blue food: blue sweet potatoes, blue dasheen, yams, edoes. No chemicals; just good food dug out of our rich, natural Caribbean earth." Coconuts were also a big sell in America, he explained. Coconut water, coconut oil, even coconut shampoo and coconut lotion for the face. And mangoes! Mangoes for everything, dried, chopped for chutney, covered in chocolate.

It might have been a purely business transaction for Robert, but that was why Lila loved him. Robert was an ardent defender of Caribbean culture, Caribbean music, Caribbean food. He had defended her against the slanderous suggestion that she would betray her people and slavishly accede to the wishes of the colonizer. He had dismissed the note outright.

She did not expect to see Terrence or Gail at the dean's reception—neither worked in the School of Liberal Arts—but the Art Department was part of the school, so Elaine would be there.

"You can't stand or sit next to each other," Terrence had said to Lila. "It would be interpreted as if the Black faculty were cooking up some secret plot against the white faculty."

"There'll be only the two of us," Lila protested.

"Enough for a conspiracy," Terrence said.

Lila thought he was joking until it seemed to her that Elaine was in fact deliberately avoiding her at the reception. She was standing at the far end of the room, opposite to the entrance, huddled with a group of faculty. Lila started to approach her and their eyes met briefly, but before Lila could get closer, Elaine turned back. Her laughter traveled across the room as she huddled again with the people around her. She would play along, Lila decided. She would focus on checking out Robert's theory. Could it be possible that the perfumed oil had come from a jealous faculty member and not from Terrence? All the faculty from the School of Liberal Arts would be at the reception. The gathering would be her best chance to find out whether that could be true or not. When she had first entered the room, she thought she detected a whiff of the oil. The scent was faint, barely detectable, and she would have pursued its trail had she not been distracted when she spotted Elaine across the room. Now she wondered whether she had indeed smelled the perfume. She was sniffing again, discretely she hoped, when she felt a hand on her arm.

It was Dr. Campbell. "Something wrong, Lila? Do you have a cold?"

Lila was mortified. She had just leaned close to the man in front of her and sniffed his jacket. Like a bunny rabbit, Lila was ashamed to admit to herself. Dr. Campbell was laughing at her, mocking her; the smile on her lips was not sincere.

Lila took out a tissue from her handbag and dabbed her nose. "Allergies," she said. "Nothing serious."

"If you need something . . ." Dr. Campbell offered.

"Oh, not at all. My nose. It was itching."

"Probably the dry air. It happens in the winter. When the heat comes on, it sucks out all the moisture from the room. It can be uncomfortable."

Lila relaxed.

"Come." Dr. Campbell took her hand. "The dean wants to introduce you to the rest of the faculty."

He was a plain-looking man, lips barely visible, a short nose, brown eyes. He was fairly young, in his late thirties, already growing bald. But he had the body of an athlete, broad shoulders, slim waist, sturdy legs. She had heard that he ran ten miles every day. They had met before and Lila braced herself for his firm handshake.

"Good, good," he said, finally releasing her hand. "I want everyone to meet you." He clapped his hands and called the faculty to attention. Lila glanced at the corner where Elaine was now talking to a group of women.

Elaine turned, and avoiding eye contact with Lila, fixed her gaze on the dean.

"Dr. Lila Bonnard," the dean said, opening his hands toward Lila in a gesture of greeting, and bowing slightly. "I know she doesn't need any introduction to the English faculty, and perhaps not to the rest of you, but I want to welcome her formally to the School of Liberal Arts."

The dean spoke of Lila's accomplishments, especially her work that had brought her to Mayfield. Perhaps he had been advised by Dr. Campbell not to dwell on her essay on appropriation. It was not a subject that would be wise for him to raise when there were questions as to whether Ron was targeted because he was Black. He said only that Dr. Bonnard had given the English Department a fresh look at Shakespeare's *The Tempest*.

The faculty applauded.

Later, one of the English faculty, Marie Henley, introduced her to a small group who seemed anxious to meet her. Lila liked Marie; she was a bone-thin woman with a nervous tick that made her appear to be smiling even when she wasn't. They never seemed to meet outside of the college grounds, though Lila was sure she had recognized her more than once when she was shopping in the grocery store. Still, they exchanged pleasantries in the corridors of the college or if they happened to see each other on the pathways.

"Dr. Lila Bonnard," Marie Henley said. "PhD from Oxford University."

Perhaps it was the way Marie Henley beamed, as if she were introducing some world-renowned scholar— her smile exaggerated because of her nervous tick—that seemed to irritate the tall, impressive-looking professor who was standing among them. He smirked and drew his hand through his thick blond hair. "Graham Adams," he said. "No need for titles."

"Oh, don't be so modest," Marie protested. "Graham here is a philosopher. He has a PhD from Harvard."

"To my students, my title does not matter," he said. "I'm Professor Adams to them. Or Graham, if they prefer. Whether I have a PhD from Harvard . . ." He paused and bowed slightly at Lila, "or Oxford, it's of no concern to them. What matters is what I teach them."

Lila felt his comment was directed at her, at the fuss the dean had made about her credentials and the way Marie Henley had introduced her. She excused herself after a brief exchange and mingled with other faculty.

Lila saw Terrence in the hallway the next day. He stopped when he reached her, shook his head, and wagged his finger at her. Elaine had told him about Lila's interaction with Graham Adams. Lila had not seen when Elaine left the reception, but she did notice that she was not far away when Marie Henley was introducing her to Adams.

"He's a pompous ass," Terrence said. "He's not a fool, though. He knows what he's doing. It's an affectation meant to make the faculty feel inferior. We don't get much money for what we do; teaching is low on the financial totem pole. But we get status, clout, respect. That is what Graham wants. He pretends he doesn't care, but he knows that he raises curiosity. Someone will ask, someone will find out, and then they will praise him for his humility, which is not humility at all; it's pride, hubris. He knows the awe the mere mention of

Harvard instills in people. *Harvard? Only geniuses go to Harvard!* They won't make the mistake of calling him Graham. Or if they do, they will know he has accorded them a special privilege and they will feel beholden to him, even more inferior. But you, Lila, do not have the luxury he has of pretending. People assume that the Black faculty got where they are because of some affirmative action quota. All of us—all Black faculty—work under that cloud of suspicion. Even the students suspect us. They ask us stupid questions just to catch us making a mistake. Tell me, Lila, didn't you notice this when you taught your first class?"

Lila reflected on her first class. There was that boy with the iPhone disrupting the class with his announcement that Bob Marley was a drug addict, and when she didn't respond, he tried to discredit the entire island. Jamaica has one of the highest murder rates in the world, he said. Then there was the student who belted out a Rihanna song and the laughter that followed.

"They don't take us seriously until we can prove to them that we have the credentials," Terrence was saying.

"I suppose the students here are different from the ones I taught back home," Lila said.

"How different?"

"I find their attitude more casual." She was not prepared to accept Terrence's dismal outlook. Those incidents happened on the first day. They were not repeated. How could she teach students who doubted her command of her subject? "They seem more playful," she added.

"Not with all the professors, I assure you," Terrence

said. "Like a police officer with a search warrant, we have to show them our badge before they let us in. So you tell them, Lila; you say you are Dr. Bonnard, and your degree is from Oxford. That will blow them away. Blow away the students *and* the faculty. That's what blew away Graham. I'm sure he looked up your credentials when you came to Mayfield. Oxford? Only geniuses go to Oxford!"

26

She was in a good mood when Gail called to invite her to dinner. Terrence had complimented her. *Only geniuses go to Oxford!*

The dinner invitation was Terrence's idea, Gail said. Elaine would be there too. "There's an Indian restaurant just outside Mayfield," Gail explained. "Terrence thought you'd like to go there."

"I hope he's not mixing up West Indian with Indian," Lila said lightly. "I'm not Indian."

Gail laughed. "We know about the mistake Columbus made. Not all Americans are ignorant about the history of the rest of the world. But if you ask me, there are so many Indians in the West Indies with ancestors from India, they could probably legitimately lay claim to the name."

"Funny," said Lila.

"But true, wouldn't you say?"

"I'd say my island is in the Caribbean Sea, named after the Carib Amerindians who were the original inhabitants of the land before the Europeans wiped out most of them with small pox and slaughtered the rest."

"Touché," said Gail. "About dinner, I'll drive you there. Terrence will be coming in a separate car with Elaine."

"Not shutting me out again, I hope," Lila said jokingly, though she was serious too.

"We want to get together with you," Gail said. "We want to take you out for a nice dinner in a nice restaurant. Anyhow, it'll give us a chance to talk. We want to know more about you. Your family. And that fiancé. What's his name again?"

"Robert."

"We want to know about Robert."

Lila was not convinced. Still, she wanted to go.

The dinner was the next evening and Lila fussed over what to wear. Nothing too formal, she thought. Something dressy, something that would send the message that she was happy to see them, even if she was also nervous. Terrence had not pressured her to say affirmatively what she would do, but at the restaurant, surrounded by his friends, would he shame her into promising to join their side, make her feel guilty for not reporting to the police what she had seen?

She reached into her closet and pulled out a black knit dress with white polka dots. She had not yet grown accustomed to the grays, blacks, and browns the fall season seemed to demand. On her island, grays, blacks, and browns were colors she would wear to a funeral, but the white polka dots on this dress would relieve the somberness of the heavy black material, and the white linen collar at the neck would brighten her face.

"I'd be careful," Robert had said when she called several hours earlier to tell him about the invitation. "Remember that note under your door?"

"Weren't you the one who told me it couldn't have been Terrence who put it there? Didn't you say it could have been any of the faculty in the department? And there I was at the dean's reception sniffing that poor man's jacket like an idiot."

"You smelled the perfume, didn't you?"

"The scent faded. I couldn't be sure. It was probably my imagination playing tricks on me. Anyhow, as you said, it couldn't have been Terrence. And surely you don't suspect Elaine or Gail?"

"You're still an outsider to them, Lila. Don't forget that. They need you now for their case against that policeman. That's all this dinner is about. Don't go thinking that they won't exclude you again when it's expedient. I know you want to be friends with them . . ."

She did want their friendship. She was beginning to feel lonely, her life oscillating between teaching and solitary hours in her room or at a café having meals by herself, only occasionally exchanging brief conversations with the other professors, and almost always at faculty meetings. No one so far had invited her to their home. And she dared not go uninvited. There were unspoken rules, conventions, and traditions she had to abide by. She had already been told by friends who had been to America that one could not just drop by a friend's place. In America, one had to be invited, or at least one had to announce one's intention to visit, sometimes days beforehand. In America one made dates, arranged dates for visits, even with a friend.

How many times had her grandmother set the table for the two of them and then a friend dropped by uninvited? No one complained. In fact, the friend was always welcomed warmly, plates and silverware brought out.

"It's another difference," Robert had said to her weeks ago, "that proves my point. We are not the same.

Americans think the individual is more important than the community. With us, the community matters just as much, if not more."

And wasn't that Terrence's argument too? Hadn't he wanted her to put aside her concerns for her personal well-being for the sake of helping to bring justice to the Black community?

"Be careful, Lila," Robert had repeated in a more compassionate tone. "Don't raise your expectations. I don't want you to get hurt."

"I think it's pretty nice of them to invite me to dinner," she had said. "They didn't have to."

"Then just remember not to get involved. It's their business, their problem."

Lila had put down the phone. Robert had dampened her mood, but he was wrong. It was her business too, her problem too.

She put back the black polka dot dress. She would wear something light and pretty, and she would smile when she saw Terrence and Elaine. At the far end of the closet, pushed tightly together, were the clothes she had brought with her from her island, brightly colored dresses, their fabric airy. She pulled out her favorite, a red sleeveless silk dress. She would wear a navy jacket over it and leave the jacket unbuttoned.

At the restaurant, they took a table near the large window where there was a clear view of the pathway that led to the front door. Lila wanted to see whether Gail's optimism was well founded or simply what she hoped. If Terrence and Elaine were walking slowly as they approached the restaurant, it would be a sign that they were not looking forward to the evening. The expressions on their faces would tell all, whether they were genuinely happy to have dinner with her, or—and she whisked away the thought as quickly as it came—that Robert had correctly guessed their motivation.

She was relieved when she finally spotted them. They were chatting happily with each other. At one point Terrence put his hand on Elaine's arm. Whatever he said seemed to please her. She did not remove his hand and her face lit up with a broad smile. Elaine had worn a black pants suit at the dean's reception. Her hair had been pulled in a severe bun at the back of her neck. Now it was braided, the ends of the locks brushing against her shoulders. She was dressed in the colors Lila had admired when they first met. She had on a coat of course, but it was short, barely reaching above her knees, and below the coat was a long skirt that grazed the tops of her shoes. From where she sat, Lila could not determine the material of the skirt—it seemed to her to be cotton—but she was familiar with the colors; they were the colors of kente cloth—oranges, reds, yellows, deep blues, greens woven together in intricate patterns, a design quintessentially Ghanian

"They're coming. I can see them." Lila slipped off her jacket.

Gail frowned. "I think you should put your jacket back on. This is not the Caribbean. It gets chilly in here."

"Look at what Elaine's wearing," Lila said. "It looks like cotton."

"Wait till she takes off her coat," Gail said.

Elaine handed her coat to Terrence at the coat check at the entrance of the restaurant, and as she was approaching them, Lila could see that under her coat Elaine had indeed worn something warm and snug. She had on a cotton skirt but she had also worn a turtleneck with long sleeves that covered the length of her arms.

Gail glanced at Lila and shook her head as if to say, *I told you so.* Lila shrugged and stood up to greet Elaine who was walking swiftly toward them, her arms wide open. "I'm so sorry I missed you at the dean's reception, Lila. There were so many people around you. I didn't want to interfere. But I'm here now." She folded Lila into her arms and pulled her against her chest. Immediately Lila stiffened. *Her perfume!*

Elaine didn't seem to notice Lila's reaction. She released Lila and stroked her arm. Like a robot, an automaton, Lila swung her arm back and Elaine's hand slipped off. By now, Gail had braced herself on her chair and was getting up to greet Elaine.

Elaine stopped her. "No. Sit," she said, and leaned down to hug Gail.

Gail flinched, almost imperceptibly, but Lila saw her shoulders jerk stiffly backward and the slight shudder that ran down her back. *She smells the perfume too.*

"Good to see you, Gail." Elaine pulled out the chair next to Gail. "Terrence is just putting away my coat. Let's all sit." But Lila didn't move. "He'll be here in a moment. You don't have to stay standing. Sit."

"I can't . . ." Lila looked helplessly at Gail.

"Can't?" Elaine wrinkled her forehead. "What's the matter?" She stretched out her hand to touch Lila's arm. Lila reared back.

"What?" Elaine spun her head from Lila to Gail and

back again. "What is it? What's the matter, Lila?"

Lila could not find her voice. Her knees felt weak and a cold sweat began to snake up her neck. She swayed and Gail moved quickly to slip her hand under Lila's elbow and hold her up. "I'll take her to the restroom," she said. "Must be something she ate." She held up her hand when Elaine offered to help. "No!" she said. "Wait for us. We'll be back."

In the restroom, Gail pulled down the lid over the toilet bowl and eased Lila onto it. "Here, put your head between your knees. You'll feel better."

"Why?" The word came out from Lila's lips in a hoarse whisper. "What have I ever done to her?"

"You can't be sure, Lila. Don't jump to conclusions before you have proof."

"I saw you flinch. I know you smelled it too."

"Many Black women use that perfume," Gail said.

"You said . . ." Lila looked up at her; her eyes were red-rimmed. "You told me . . ."

"I know. But look at what Elaine is wearing. It's an African-style dress."

"Kente cloth," Lila murmured.

"Precisely. So she'd want to use a scent from Africa. To match her dress."

Lila swiped her nose with the back of her hand. "I thought it would have been one of Terrence's students. I thought Terrence had got them all riled up about me. All those books in his office. He would have had his students read Fanon. And one of them—"

"That's not you, Lila. Fanon was not writing about you."

"All that boy knew was that I speak with a Caribbean accent. So I must be one of those puppets . . ."

"Don't do this to yourself, Lila." Gail pulled out a bunch of paper towels from the metal dispenser attached to the wall. She soaked them under the sink and wrung them out. "Here. Let me." She put the wet towels on Lila's forehead. "It'll cool you down."

Lila grimaced. "Then I thought it wasn't the boy. It was someone in the department who didn't like how I was changing the curriculum. I never thought it would be Elaine."

"It may not have been Elaine. It could have been anyone. Someone playing a prank on you."

"A prank? Who would do that, Gail? Who? Elaine avoided me at the dean's reception. She saw I was looking at her, about to approach her, and she turned her back on me. I should have suspected her then, but Terrence had told me some foolishness about a conspiracy."

"What conspiracy?"

"He said that when white people see a group of Black people huddled together talking, they assume the Black people are planning something against them."

Gail shook her head dismissively and removed the wet paper towels from Lila's forehead. "Do you think you can stand?"

"I'm a bit shaky."

"You can hold onto me," Gail said and helped her up.

Lila wobbled slightly and clutched Gail's hand. "I thought I smelled the perfume when I came into the room at the dean's reception," she said, steadying herself. "And Elaine had been standing there, near the door.

The scent faded, but that was because Elaine went to the far side of the room."

"You may be wrong, Lila. I just don't think you can pin that note on Elaine because she avoided you at the dean's reception."

"So you agree with Terrence?" Lila let go of Gail's hand. "You think Elaine was avoiding me because she didn't want to scare the white faculty, give them the wrong impression?"

"Terrence wasn't serious. But there's history here you haven't experienced." Gail paused as if anticipating Lila's reaction, and when Lila said nothing, she added more forcefully, "It still could have been the boy, Terrence's student."

"Elaine smelled of the same scent as the note," Lila said firmly. "I know you smelled it too."

"Okay. I'll grant you that the scents are similar, but if Elaine put that note under your door, why would she wear the same scent when she knew she would be meeting you here? What would be her motive?"

"I don't know."

"That's it precisely. You don't know. So it doesn't make sense to accuse her."

"Maybe she was sending me a warning," Lila said.

"A warning about what?"

"I don't know."

"You don't know and I don't know. So put that thought out of your head. Elaine is only wearing a perfume to match her outfit. She likes African things."

A dull pain spread across the front of Lila's head and beat against the back of her eyes. "I can't go back there," she said.

"What do you want to do?"

"I can't face her."

"It may not have been her," Gail said again.

"I won't have dinner with her."

"Then you'll have to pretend."

"I won't have to pretend. I feel sick," Lila said

"What should I say?"

"You told them I might have eaten something that made me sick. Tell them that again."

Gail went back to the dining room and made excuses for Lila. She got their coats and returned to the restroom. Elaine and Terrence stood up when she and Lila passed them. Lila could hear Elaine muttering something in a sad voice but she kept her head down on the way out.

27

Terrence knocked on her door. "Lunch?" Lila had just returned from her class. Thankfully, she had had the weekend to recover, to take control of her emotions. On the drive back to Mrs. Lowell's house, Gail had continued trying to dissuade her from blaming Elaine. Elaine is a good person, Gail said. She would never have wanted to hurt her. Elaine had looked forward to her arrival at Mayfield. She had told Gail all about Lila's essay, about the Olympics in London, about the Englishmen on the hill. Elaine was proud of her.

Lila listened as Gail repeated the explanation she had offered before: it could have been a student playing a prank on her. Yet Lila could not shake out of her mind the possibility—no, the probability—that it was Elaine who had put the note under her door.

"I was worried about you," Terrence said when Lila invited him in. "I called, but Mrs. Lowell said you were resting."

Lila was not surprised he had come to her office. Mrs. Lowell had told her he called. Three times.

She began packing her books and her student papers in her briefcase. "It's lunchtime," she said. "I'm about to go home."

Terrence held up a brown paper bag. "I brought lunch. I thought we could eat by the lake."

"Too cold for me," Lila said, and snapped her briefcase shut.

"Look, I don't know what happened on Friday at dinner, but I'm not dumb enough to think that you'd feel sick all of a sudden. I saw you standing at the table when we came into the restaurant. You looked fine then."

"I can't sit outside. I'm a West Indian girl, remember?" Lila looked straight at him.

Terrence winced. "I deserve that. You are a Caribbean woman. I was wrong. I apologize. I knew better."

His voice was soft and gentle, and his manner, shoulders slumped, eyes begging her forgiveness, touched her. "So?" she said. "Where to?"

He perked up. "There's a glass-enclosed shelter by the lake. It's sunny outside so the shelter should be fairly warm."

"Warm enough to take off my coat?" She was smiling when she asked the question, but there was an undercurrent of sarcasm in her tone that could not be missed.

"I'm really sorry. Only an insensitive idiot says West Indian, not Caribbean."

Lila tossed her head and waved him away. "I was talking about the weather. It's fall, not summer."

"Ha!" He rolled his hands over each other. "Ha!" he repeated. "So you'll come with me? You'd be surprised how warm it is in the shelter. They put solar panels on the roof. Hard to believe, but even small Mayfield is experimenting with solar energy."

She was curious about what he had to say to her, less so about the newfangled solar panels (new anyway to Mayfield) that were popping up on the roofs of some of the houses.

"Okay," she said. "Lunch by the lake."

On the way there, they studiously avoided any comments that could revive the tension that had flared up and had thankfully quickly subsided, Terrence asking her anodyne questions: How was she adjusting to the change in the seasons? You have only one season on your island, right? Two, she said, answering him in the same benign conversational tone. She told him about the giant blossoming trees in the dry season—the poui, the flamboyant, the immortelle—and the rhyme she learned as a child about the coming of the rainy season: *June too soon, July stand by, August come it must, September remember, October all over*. He laughed and seemed to relax. He asked about her classes, about the literature she was teaching. He seemed interested, but when she paused, he gave no indication that he wanted her to continue telling him about Kincaid or Hodge or Powell, or about the literature of any of the other Caribbean women writers. Instead, he fixed his eyes on the road and began naming the streets they were passing. Twenty minutes later, they were at the lake.

"It was built recently. The students haven't discovered it yet," he said. "We'll probably be the only people there. Wait till the spring when the students find it! There won't be any space for us to sit."

They had to walk along a narrow path from the street to where the glass-enclosed shelter with its newfangled solar roof stood on a small incline that sloped down to the lake and was fenced off from the row of houses behind it. As Terrence had predicted, the shelter was empty. There were five rows of metal benches arranged like bleachers. They sat on the top one. Before them, the lake glittered with sunlight. Terrence took off his coat. Though it was warm as he had promised, Lila only unbuttoned hers.

Terrence opened the paper bag he'd brought with him and handed her a sandwich. "It's ham and cheese. They didn't have turkey and cheese. I wanted to get what you like . . ."

Is he trying to taunt me? But there was no hint of disingenuousness in his expression, and Lila dismissed the thought that had snuck up on her. "Thanks," she said.

"I have brownies too. And apple juice. You drink apple juice?"

Lila put down her sandwich. "Why did you bring me here?"

"Don't you like the view?"

"You seemed to imply I was faking it at the restaurant. That I wasn't really sick."

"What was it? What happened?"

"Elaine," Lila said. He wanted the truth; she would give him the truth. "Her perfume." And she told him about the note, about the scent on it.

Terrence sighed. A rush of air poured through his mouth and he tugged at his chin. He didn't argue with her, or attempt to tell her she was wrong to suspect Elaine. "I didn't think she would do something like that," he said. "But I knew she was upset with you."

"Upset with me? Why?"

He sighed again. "Elaine was in love with Ron."

"In love with Ron?" Lila exclaimed. "She never said . . . never gave any indication . . ."

"That is Elaine. She is a master—I guess you'd say a mistress. She is a mistress of discretion." Terrence scratched the back of his head.

"I thought Adriana and Ron—"

"Elaine knew about Adriana and Ron."

"She knew?"

"She couldn't handle it. Ron's relationship with Adriana was too much for her."

"But why would she be angry with *me*? I didn't do anything to her."

"She thought you could have helped."

"Helped?"

"She wanted the police to pay for what they had done to Ron. She thought you should have told the police what you knew."

"And for that, she sent me an anonymous nasty note?"

"It was her way of striking back."

"And what about what Ron did to her? Why wasn't she angry with Ron? Ron was unfaithful to her."

"I think Ron was ending his affair with Adriana when he started with Elaine." Terrence pursed his lips and twisted his head from side to side. "Elaine wanted him to break off the relationship with Adriana, but Ron was worried about Adriana. He knew she was sick."

"Addicted to heroin," Lila said flatly.

"Yes, addicted to heroin. Elaine blamed Adriana for Ron's death. If Adriana had not come to the restaurant, if she had stopped begging Ron for help . . . And then you . . . If you . . ."

"If I?" Lila raised a fist to her mouth. "If I?" she repeated. "And that was enough for her to call me a hypocrite, a puppet?"

"Bitterness was eating up Elaine. Ron's in the morgue and Adriana's in the hospital. For them, drug addiction is a disease. For us, it's a crime. They go to the hospital to recover. We go to jail or the morgue." The muscles in Terrence's jaw knotted and his lips closed in a taut line. He fixed his eyes on the water in front of them. Neither of them spoke. Finally, he looked back at her. "It's the way it is for us. For African Americans. This isn't your problem, Lila. I'll speak to Elaine. She can't understand why you won't go to the police and tell them what you saw." He turned away from her. "For that matter, neither can I."

"And this is why you brought me here?"

"You never gave me an answer," he said.

She had office hours after lunch when she was expected to be available for conferences with her students. She kept her office door open, though she knew from experience that few students took advantage of this opportunity. Perhaps for some, this close contact with their professor was too intimidating; they felt vulnerable, exposed, judged for their lack of understanding of the course material. They would rather pretend, hide their insecurities. Then there were the sycophants. They believed in the adage that the squeaky wheel gets the most grease. These students bored her. They came to her office ostensibly to let her know that they were interested in what she was teaching them, when in reality all they were concerned about was getting an A. But she always looked forward to the students who came to challenge her with questions she sometimes needed to research. For the most part, though, students were simply glad that classes had ended and they could socialize with their friends. This day, however, she was relieved that no students had come to her office yet. She had managed to evade the answer Terrence was seeking from her, but she knew he would find a way to ask again, and next time more directly. She needed time to think. There would be no going back once she decided to speak to the police. Robert would be angry; he might not forgive her.

She heard footsteps approaching her door, and thinking it was a student, she quickly opened her computer to her class notes and took out her grade book. It was Clive Lewis. She had not spoken to him since they'd had breakfast together. She was glad to see him; after Terrence's revelation about the love affair between Ron and Elaine, it was a relief to talk to someone who knew about Ron's other secret.

Clive Lewis seemed happy to see her too. He looked handsomer than she remembered. He had on slim-fitting blue jeans and a loose gray T-shirt that nevertheless outlined his firm torso and narrow waist. "I was in the neighborhood and thought I'd stop by and see how you're doing," he said.

Lila rose to shake his hand. "It's good to see you," she said.

She was conscious that he held her hand longer than seemed normal. She was conscious too that she liked the feel of his hand on hers. She was still smarting from Terrence's cold retort—*For that matter, neither can I*—and there was something comforting, reassuring when Clive's large palm folded over hers.

"I'd have come earlier. My cases in Brooklyn . . ."

She came around her desk and pointed to one of the armchairs in her office. "Sit, sit." He sat down and she took the chair facing his. "So are they going well?"

"What?"

"Your cases in Brooklyn?"

He crossed his legs and gazed vacantly down at his shoes.

"What about the case against the police officer who shot Ron Brown?" she asked.

"That case?" He looked up briefly and rubbed his knee.

"Yes."

"We're preparing for the trial."

"Here at Mayfield?"

"Yes. The trial will be in Mayfield. To be honest . . ." A soft intimacy had entered his voice. He tried to catch her eyes and she looked away, ran her hands along the sides of her dress, and pressed her fingers into her thighs, determined to take control of the slight tingling that was coursing through her fingers. "I want to be honest with you, Lila . . ." he began again.

"Honest about what?"

"You are an attractive woman, Lila." He reached forward as if for her hand, and she drew back. Suddenly she was conscious of her breasts. She was wearing a navy-blue knit sheath dress. She had a matching jacket for the dress but the heat from the radiators had made her office unbearably warm and she had taken it off. It would be awkward to put it on now.

"I don't want to be presumptuous," he said.

"Then don't be."

"Navy looks good on you. But no matter what you wear, Lila, you'd be beautiful."

She was glad the color of her skin masked the blush spreading across her face. She got up, crossed the room, and closed her office door. "You know I am engaged," she said bluntly.

"I saw your ring."

"So you know this is not appropriate."

"What isn't?"

She didn't return to the chair next to him. She walked to her desk and sat on the high-backed chair behind it.

"I was merely complimenting you," he said.

She shuffled the papers on her desk and said, "I had lunch with Terrence today."

"Good." Clive seemed unperturbed by the abrupt turn in the conversation.

"He told me that Elaine and Ron were having an affair," she said.

"Adriana knew."

"You didn't tell me that. You said Adriana had given Ron an ultimatum."

"She found out after he broke up with her. Then she became more despondent."

"Maybe Ron didn't love her," Lila said.

"She should have walked away."

"Maybe she couldn't," Lila said. "Maybe she was too much in love with him. Was Terrence angry that Ron was having an affair with Adriana? I mean, because Adriana is white?"

Clive rolled his lower lip over his teeth and released it slowly. "It's hard to tell when Terrence is angry. He keeps his feelings close to his chest. He didn't approve. I know that."

"He was angry with me," Lila said.

"With you? Why?"

"He thinks I should tell the police what I saw."

"Did he say that to you? Did he ask you to be a witness?"

"I had thought Terrence put that note under my door," she said. "Or got one of his students to do his dirty work for him."

"What note?"

After she explained, Clive asked, "Why didn't you let me know this before now?"

"You told me you were working with Terrence. On the case."

"You didn't trust me?"

"I thought it was strange that you didn't ask me to be a witness," she said. "But none of this matters now. I know Elaine did it and I know why."

Clive clasped his hands behind his head and leaned back in his chair. "Terrence, Terrence," he said.

"What?"

"He doesn't trust either of us."

"I don't understand."

"He doesn't trust me because I'm white. But he'll work with me because he needs me to help him put those officers behind bars. He doesn't trust you because you are a foreigner and haven't experienced racism in America." Clive sat upright in his chair. "Terrence was setting you up."

"Setting me up?"

"He wanted to see if you were on our side. He doesn't need you to be a witness. We have other witnesses who have come forward. They're willing to testify that Ron never threatened the officer."

As he was leaving, Clive asked if she would have dinner with him. "Perhaps another time," she said, and shook his hand.

* * *

Mrs. Lowell met her at the front door with a letter in her hand. "For you," she said. Lila recognized the stamps from her island. Only her grandmother still used that old-fashioned method of communication. Lila had tried to persuade her to use e-mail, but her grandmother resisted. She said e-mail seemed like black magic to her. She could understand paper and pen, she said; they were tangible materials she could touch and see. She could understand the postal service. You put a letter in the mailbox, the postman collects it, deposits it to the post office, the post office ships it to another post office . . .

Lila opened the letter in her room. Her grandmother had good news: She had made a 180-degree turn in her attitude toward Lila's marriage to Robert. She had not changed her beliefs but she had found an exception in Lila's situation. Lila's marriage to Robert would have her blessing.

The letter began with reports about her friends: who was sick, who was in a retirement home, who had Alzheimer's (*God forbid that should happen to me! Don't let me be a burden to you, Lila. Put me in a nursing home*). There was more news about two of her friends who had died (*Life is short, enjoy it while you can*). And this advice led to her new revelations about Robert and her wish to see them married. She wrote:

Yesterday Robert came to see me. What a good-looking man he is! Such a clear complexion! I know you'll jump on me and say I like fair people, but am I so different from anyone else? It may be unfair but it's the way of the world. Life is easier when you are fair-skinned, and when you and Robert marry, you'll have fair-skinned children. Then you'll see how doors will open more easily for them than if you had married that boy.

That boy was the very dark-skinned Kenton. Lila read on:

I don't have a prejudiced bone in my body, but experience has shown me that people have a better chance for happiness if they marry their own sort. There'll be no conflict about colour in your family.

Well, to the reason Robert came to see me. He is Catholic, as you know. And I could have no objections in the world to your marrying a Catholic, but I understood he was divorced and that was a big problem. What he told me when he came yesterday changed everything. He said he got married in the courthouse. Did you know that? He must have told you. Why didn't you tell me? I was suffering so for you. His whole family is Catholic and I didn't doubt he'd marry in the Catholic Church. But he confessed that his first wife wasn't Catholic and to please her, he married her in the courthouse. A justice of the peace married them! A judge, not a priest! So now we can have a big wedding, a big Catholic Church wedding. Robert said you'll be back for Christmas. We can make our plans then.

I'm so happy.

Your loving Granny

He lied. Her poor grandmother, so gullible! Robert's first wife was Catholic, and he married her in the Catholic Church.

And yet, and yet . . .

Lila drew the letter to her chest. She felt a burst of joy and relief. Robert had lied for her; he had lied because he loved her and wanted to marry her. He would not abandon her for doing the right thing. She would tell him when the time was right, after she had gone to the police.

28

The next day, as Lila was leaving her office, Terrence approached her. They were standing in the hallway, which at that time in the evening was fairly empty. Most classes were over for the day and many of the professors had already gone home. "Ron was killed because he was a Black body," Terrence said, as if stating a fact he dared her to contradict. "I want you to know that."

Lila looked steadily at him. "Ron has a body," she responded. "Or had. But he was much more than a body."

"To you, to me," Terrence said. "Not to white people."

Lila looked down the hallway; no one was there. "You can't believe *all* white people think that way."

"Most," he said.

"Is this about Adriana and Ron? Because if it is, you must know that to Adriana, Ron was more than a body. He may not have loved her, but Adriana loved him. To her, Ron was a human being with a body, a mind, a soul."

"Ron made a mistake."

Lila fired back: "I think Adriana was the one who made a mistake."

Terrence seemed taken aback by her bold response. His eyes widened and his nostrils flared.

"Love has a way of bridging differences," Lila said, modulating her voice.

"You speak like Gail."

"Gail is a kind person," Lila said.

"Come." Terrence touched her arm lightly. "Let's walk down to my office."

They had not gone far when he stopped suddenly and said, "Okay, I sometimes get carried away. Maybe she loved him and maybe he loved her. And maybe I could have made life easier for Ron." He shook his head. "I gave him a hard time. *Where's your Blackness?* I asked him. *Where's your loyalty to Black people, Black women?*" He paused but Lila remained silent. "I thought . . . I hoped it was a passing fancy. I hoped it would blow over."

He looked so downcast that Lila pitied him. "Perhaps you are right," she said. "Perhaps that was all it was, a passing fancy. If Ron loved Adriana, he would not have broken up with her. He was probably attracted to Elaine all along, and when he was free . . . you know what they say: all's fair in love and war."

"Yes, yes. All's fair." Terrence exhaled, even venturing a smile, and began walking again. As they got closer to his office, however, he cleared his throat and took her back to his original point: "I agree that to Adriana, Ron was more than a body, but you have to understand, Lila, that to the white police officer who shot Ron, Ron was not a man in the way you and I think of a man. To him, Ron did not have feelings, thoughts, desires."

"Surely you can't say the same for all white police officers."

"Maybe not all."

"You teach here. At Mayfield. The students are white."

"I don't see them as white bodies. I see them as students who are here to learn. In any case, the job pays well."

"The job?"

"Don't get me wrong. I'm a teacher. I want my students, all of them, to achieve their potential, go further if possible. I like what I do. Of course, I'd prefer to teach Black students, but there aren't many jobs for Black professors in my field."

They had reached his office. He opened the door and she followed him inside. She was amazed once more by the piles of books scattered everywhere, on the floor, on the chairs, on his desk. He walked directly to his desk and picked up a book: *A Different Drummer* by William Melvin Kelley. "Here," he said. "You'll understand us better when you read this novel, and hopefully you'll realize that I'm not as unreasonable or as cold-hearted as you probably think I am."

He told her the novel was about an African American man named Tucker Caliban; she was immediately interested.

Back in her room at Mrs. Lowell's, Lila read the novel quickly, so riveted by the tale that she could not put it down. It was well past two in the morning when she finished. She had to admit that Terrence was neither cold-hearted nor unreasonable—the novel had indeed helped to clarify his feelings and attitudes.

Shakespeare's Caliban claimed his right to be his own king on the island that was his, passed down to him from his mother. Caribbean writers, regardless of the languages of the Europeans who colonized their islands—Aimé Césaire from Francophone Martinique;

Roberto Fernández Retamar from Spanish-speaking Cuba; George Lamming from Anglophone Barbados—all seized on Caliban's outcry: *This island's mine, by Sycorax my mother.* The Caribbean islands belong to us, they wrote defiantly, handed down to our people by the generations who have lived here. Your people have *occupied* our islands; they have not loved our islands. They have not planted roots here; they have not *lived* here, married, raised children *here*, their bodies have not returned to the earth *here*. Like Caliban, we will fight for our independence to reclaim what is rightfully ours.

But Kelley's Tucker Caliban poured salt on his land; he shot his horse and his cow; he burned down his house. He took his wife and children and the few possessions he owned, mostly clothes, and left town. All his African American neighbors followed him.

For the whites, this deliberate destruction of property and the strange exodus from the town were a mystery they were incapable of unraveling. Why, when Tucker Caliban had everything going for him—white employers who treated him kindly and fairly, land that he was able to purchase from his wages, a farm that produced income to provide his family with food and shelter— why would he abandon his job, poison his land, kill his livestock, burn down his house?

By the time Lila closed the book, she knew the answer. The land was not his and so the livestock was not his, the house was not his. His memory was long; he could not forget that *his* land was stolen from his people in Africa.

Kelley had created a different Caliban from the Caribbean Caliban that Césaire, Retamar, and Lamming wrote about. Kelley's Caliban was uniquely American, an African American Caliban. He was the descendant of men and women stripped from their homelands in Africa and brought to labor under the lash in a foreign land where white people lived, having already seized the land from the original inhabitants.

Lila's throat was parched. She filled a glass with water and drained it. She opened her laptop and e-mailed Terrence.

I have to concede that on my island we did not suffer the intensity of the brutal assault on our bodies for as long as your people did. (And on our spirits, you will add. For more than four hundred years.) We have not experienced your level of racial inequality that threatens to strip away our confidence in our abilities, our talents, our beauty. (Here, I know, you will correct me. Not have experienced, you'll say; still experience, you'll say.) We have not had to endure the constant effort by some white people to deem us inferior human beings. (You will name Nobel laureate William Shockley; you will name Charles Murray and his book "The Bell Curve.") The color of our skin does not make us a target for the police. (You will list the names of Black men shot down like dogs by the police. Even today. Black men are an endangered species, you will say.)

So what do you want? What does Tucker Caliban want?

Before she struck the send button, Lila gave him her answer to the questions she asked. *Reparations*, she wrote.

It was the darkest hour of the morning and Terrence

presumably should be sleeping, but he answered her immediately: *Well, Lila, now you know.*

29

Robert laughed. "Reparations? It's too late for that, Lila."

"'May one be pardon'd and retain th' offense?'" Lila intoned.

"What's that?"

"*Hamlet*. Claudius's prayer."

Robert coughed. There was a pause on the phone. It didn't last long. But Lila was ready with a new approach. "It wasn't too late to give reparations to the Jews," she said.

"The Holocaust happened within the memory of people who are still alive," Robert said. "You don't see people arguing for reparations for the slavery of the Jewish people in Egypt."

"Because the Jewish people were given Israel."

"Because Israel was historically theirs," Robert said.

"For the Palestinians that is debatable. *Historically*."

Robert was silent.

"And yet Israel gets money from America," Lila continued.

"I don't see it that way," Robert said. "It's in America's national security interest to have a partner in the Middle East."

"Then what about the Japanese?"

"You can't mean the Japanese in Japan, Lila?"

"They too. America helped rebuild their country."

"That was not reparations. America bombed Naga-saki and Hiroshima. America decimated those places."

"Exactly my point," Lila said. "America made repa-rations for what it had done."

"I don't think the American government had repara-tions in mind. I think they viewed rebuilding Japan as insurance against attack from the East. Having an ally in Asia."

"Then what about the Japanese Americans who were put into concentration camps in America during World War II?"

Silence.

"Japanese Americans were given reparations," Lila said.

Silence again.

Lila pressed her point: "And the Germans continue to give reparations to the relatives of Jews no matter where they live in the world."

"So what do you want, Lila? Reparations for slavery in America?"

"It happened on our islands too. And white people—the slave owners—were given reparations when slavery ended. They got land. Lots of land. Compensation for the loss of labor." Lila snorted. "Free labor on the backs of Africans. Land *and* twenty million British pounds. That's what they got. You know how much that is in to-day's money? More than twenty billion. *Billion*, Robert."

Robert sighed. "And what would be fair? Would it be fair to give money to *every single Black person* to compen-sate for the enslavement of their ancestors?"

Lila repeated Claudius's prayer.

* * *

"A red herring," Terrence said when Lila presented Robert's arguments to him. "The solution is simple. Provide resources so that every Black person can get a decent education. Education is the key. Teach a man to fish and he'll be a fisherman."

30

She ran into Terrence a few days later as he was walking to class. He was glad to see her, he said. "Things are heating up on campus. There's going to be a protest march." Where? When? she asked. "You can't join," he said. Her work visa, etcetera, he explained. "I don't want you to jeopardize your future here. We need you. The students need you."

His attitude had changed dramatically since she'd sent him that e-mail after reading Melvin Kelley's novel. Lately he'd begun to assume the role of her protector. "To help you navigate the minefields in white America," he said.

Still, she wanted to go. A book, a story, and it had changed her. She was an elitist, Kenton said. She had pursued a frivolous academic degree. How could a degree in literature change the world, make it better? But he was wrong. There was power in fiction, in the catharsis story made possible. Catharsis had opened her heart to feelings and feelings had led her to a desire to act.

"I want to march too," she said.

"Not wise. There's an anti-immigrant wave sweeping this country," Terrence said. "Brown and Black immigrants are especially targeted. You have to be careful not to give them any excuse to deport you."

"I'm just a professor," she said.

"A *Black* professor," Terrence said firmly, but without rancor.

Not very long ago she would have agreed with Robert that the adjective was unnecessary, but she was quickly beginning to understand the importance of tribes, of the possible loss or gain if you were outside or inside a tribe. A Black person needs an army of supporters when there is trouble, the killing of an innocent Black man, for example.

If she were asked, when she was on her island, whether professors should remain neutral and not get involved in politics, she would have said yes. That is what she'd thought when she heard that a group of American professors had signed a petition demanding that Toni Morrison be awarded the National Book Award for her novel *Beloved*. The great Toni Morrison should not have needed an army, but Lila was now convinced that without that army of professors, the arbiters of the Pulitzer Prize and the National Book Award would have continued to disregard her work, as they had disregarded her previous masterpieces: *The Bluest Eye*, *Sula*, *Song of Solomon*, *Tar Baby*. And in the end, didn't a panel of international judges award Toni Morrison the Nobel Prize?

Yes, here in America, it was important to remember she was a Black professor.

"Your dark skin makes you a threat," Terrence was saying. "White America is afraid to let more of you in here. You can get married—"

"Here? I plan to get married back home and live there."

"Well, ICE . . ."

She frowned.

"The Immigration and Customs Enforcement federal agency," he continued. "They aren't about to take that chance. You could change your mind, decide to stay, get married and have Black and brown babies, and then the balance of the population will get turned upside down. Already demographers are saying that in a few years there'll be more brown and Black people in America than white people. Or just the same percentage. White people are afraid of what could happen when those numbers switch. Some of them won't give up so easily. As Frederick Douglass warned us: 'Power concedes nothing without a demand. It never did and it never will.' So keep your head down, Lila."

"Didn't you tell me you wanted me to be a witness?"

Terrence grinned.

"Clive said you didn't need me after all. There were other witnesses."

"Just testing you," Terrence said.

"And what's my grade?"

"Passed with flying colors. A+."

Lila shook her head and narrowed her eyes. "Well, I still intend to be a witness."

It was still dark when Lila left her apartment the morning of the march. She went directly to her office. She would be safer there, she thought, out of sight of curious eyes who might want to know why she had not joined her colleagues. She felt like a coward, a sneak, as she tiptoed up the front steps of her building, but Terrence's advice was reverberating in her ears. She didn't think she was at risk of having her visa revoked, but Terrence had warned her there were always plants who join a protest march for the sole purpose of spying for the government. "Think Nixon," he said. Nixon had spies infiltrate the crowds protesting against him, he told her. It was hard to recognize them; they looked like beatniks, just like the other marchers—long hair, headbands, bell-bottom jeans, flowered skirts, flowers everywhere. They took down the names of the troublemakers. "It wouldn't be good to be on a government list of troublemakers," Terrence said, "even if you were simply exercising your First Amendment rights." Then he frightened her some more: "Oh no, I forgot!" What he forgot, he explained, was that she had no such protection since she was not an American citizen. The First Amendment did not apply to her.

Still, if it was unwise for her to go, she at least wanted to see the march.

The window in her office overlooked the grassy circle facing the academic building where the march was scheduled to begin and end. There was a flagpole in the middle of the circle. The flag was still lowered when she arrived, but as the dawn clouds began to dissipate, a uniformed worker came out and raised it. The colors fluttered in the slight breeze—red, white, and blue, like the colors of the British flag—and it crossed Lila's mind that this too, this big powerful country, was once a colony like hers; that England, small island that it is, once ruled the world, and in America, big country that it is, people speak the English language, though some would claim only a variant of it.

A few people began milling around the flagpole. The march would not start until midmorning, so Lila opened the book she had brought with her and settled down comfortably in her armchair. She had left her office door slightly ajar. It was her single concession to herself, a false reassurance (she was honest enough to admit it) that she was not so afraid that she would lock herself up in her office. If anyone wanted to come in, they were free to do so. She was not in hiding.

About eleven o'clock, the protest began. She heard the shouts coming from a megaphone: *Black Lives Matter!* She closed the book she was reading and went to the window. She counted the numbers. Less than twenty-five. The two Black faculty were there—Terrence and Elaine. Gail was there too, the only Black member of Mayfield's staff. Students who were walking to class or simply hanging out chatting with friends paused to cheer on the protesters with loud applause and calls of encouragement: *Way to go!* But none of them repeated the chant of *Black Lives Matter*. Standing on the sidewalk was a small group of white faculty; they too did not join the chant.

"Hi there!" Clive Lewis was standing in her doorway, dressed casually in sweater and jeans, greeting her as if it were an ordinary Saturday. She was glad that she was dressed casually as well, in a sweater and skirt, though she had almost reached for her suit jacket. He had a steaming paper cup in one hand and a brown bag in the other. "I brought you breakfast. Tea with milk, no sugar, as you like it."

"As I like it?"

"I observed," he said.

She frowned.

"In the café," he added.

She could have hugged him. She hadn't realized

how miserable and lonely she had been feeling, her face against the window, all of humanity, it seemed, going about its business without her.

"Brought a roll with scrambled eggs too."

She left the window and took the tea from his hand. "And for yourself?" she asked, trying hard to sound nonchalant. *He's a friend. Just a friend*, she reminded herself.

"Two rolls with scrambled eggs." He took them out of the paper bag. "One for you, one for me." He put the bag on her desk. "And I was hoping you'd share your tea."

"I don't have another cup," she said.

"Wait!" He held up his hand and dashed out the door. In less than a minute, he was back with an empty paper cup.

"Where did you get it?"

"Oh, I know my way around this building," he said, and poured some of the tea into the cup.

If Terrence's warnings had made her slightly afraid, she was no longer feeling that way. If there were spies, plants, downstairs among the marchers, Clive would know; he would protect her.

"How did you know I was here?" Lila asked. Her fingers were chilly from pressing them against the cold windowpane and she wrapped her hands around the hot paper cup.

"I saw the light in your office."

"From the corridor?"

"From downstairs. I was standing by the flagpole."

"I didn't see you."

"I noticed you looking down from the window. You turned around before I could wave."

"And you just so happened to have two rolls," she said, laughing.

"One tea, as you can see."

She didn't point out it was tea, not his usual coffee. "Come." She invited him to sit next to her and told him what Terrence had said. He agreed there were spies at protest marches, but this one was too insignificant to attract the attention of the government. "It's Mayfield. It's not as if we're in a big city."

"What about the police?" she asked. "They can't be happy about this."

"Some of them think the officer who shot Ron was a bad apple. They may be secretly glad the kids are protesting."

"I'm glad you're here," she said.

"So you'll come with me? We can go down after we eat. We have time. They'll be gathering at the flagpole for a while."

"Yes."

Someone had brought a drum. Against the measured beats that sounded to Lila like a call to arms, one of the students announced on the megaphone that the march was about to begin. Clive collected their empty paper cups and napkins, stuffed them in the paper bag, and threw everything in the trash. "Are you ready?" he asked.

She was ready, but apprehensive. Elaine was there, at the flagpole, standing next to Terrence and Gail. Elaine had intimated that Lila was a traitor, someone whose strings could be controlled by the puppeteer. By the colonizer. By the white man. By an all-white police department investigating the death of the man she loved.

She must find it in her heart to forgive Elaine, Lila

told herself. She recalled her grandmother's advice: *Forgive not for the sake of the person who offended you, but for your own sake. Don't carry the burden of the hurt and pain. Release it.*

Elaine was desperate. Her world had fallen apart when the man she loved was senselessly killed. It was love that had sparked Elaine's bitterness toward her.

Still.

Clive was walking ahead of her. Lila hung back, willing, but not ready, to forgive.

Elaine had left the group at the flagpole and was coming toward her. Her eyes were damp, her lips ashen. Lila felt her heart contract and an overpowering feeling of sympathy washed over her.

"I don't know what got in my head to do such an evil thing." Elaine was standing in front of her.

Instinctively, Lila inhaled. *No scent of the perfumed oil.*

"How I misjudged you! Can you? Will you forgive me? Terrence said . . . Terrence told me . . ."

Release it. For your own sake, don't carry the burden.

"I was afraid," Lila murmured.

"No! You were right."

"I was afraid to get involved."

"You shouldn't. This is not the time to get tangled up with the police. There's a lot of animosity these days toward immigrants. Especially brown and Black immigrants."

"Terrence said the same thing."

"Don't give them an excuse. There's a blue line in the police force."

"A blue line?"

"A loyalty test for police officers who wear the blue uniform. They hate snitches. If you make trouble for one of them, they'll go after you. Harass you. Follow you wherever you go."

"But I obey the law."

"It doesn't matter. They could make up something on you. They could plant something in your office, in your purse, in your briefcase. Marijuana. They'll say you brought marijuana from your island."

Lila's eyes opened wide.

"I don't want to scare you," Elaine said.

"I don't smoke marijuana."

"It won't matter. You should stay away from the police."

"But I was there."

"There are other witnesses."

"I can prove—"

"Don't take that chance. You are willing to be a witness. That's all that counts for me." Elaine stepped closer. "Can you forgive me? Will you let me give you a hug?"

Lila put her arms around Elaine. Over Elaine's shoulder, she could see Terrence. He was smiling.

Another apology was owing. This time Lila knew it was her turn. She had virtually accused Steve, Terrence's student, of slandering her. She had stalked him, pretending to ask him about Fanon. He had outwitted her then, and now she knew he was innocent.

At first he was indistinguishable from the other students gathered for the march near the flagpole. Like them, he was dressed all in black—black hooded jacket, black pants, black boots. It was the tattoo she recognized, the flower blooming on his neck. She would wait until the march was over, she decided.

Another rapid drumbeat. A leader called the group to order. They should line up three in a row, he said. But before the marchers could find their places, something strange happened. Lila saw Steve jostling past the students in front of him and sprinting toward the leader. "Wait!" he shouted. The leader turned around. "Wait! Something terrible. Horrible." Steve was breathing hard, sweat dripping down the sides of his face. When he reached the leader, he leaned close to him and whispered something in his ear. The leader lurched backward and clasped his hand over his eyes.

"What's happening?" Lila asked.

"Look! That young man has taken the megaphone," Gail said.

"It's Steve, the student I told you about."

Steve was whispering in the leader's ear again. Everyone was now looking at Steve, anxiously waiting for him to speak.

"Do you know what he wants to say?" Lila asked.

Terrence shrugged.

Elaine's fingers punched at her iPhone. A barrage of words in bold letters flooded the screen. She passed the iPhone to Terrence, who made a hissing sound and turned as if to leave. Elaine put her hand on his arm and stopped him. She jerked her head toward Steve, who had brought the megaphone to his mouth. "Don't go yet. Listen to what he has to say."

"I have a twelve-year-old brother," Steve began. "Like me, he is white. And because he is white, he is safe. He can play in the park with his favorite toys. He likes to play cops and robbers with his friends. They all have toy guns and all of them are safe, safe to play with their toys where and when they want." He drew in his breath and ground his teeth over his lower lip. His lip was bloodred when he released it. "This morning, a twelve-year-old boy, just like my brother, was not safe. He was playing with his toy gun, just like my brother. And he was shot, killed by the police."

Loud gasps rippled through the grounds where the marchers were gathered. Lila turned toward the faculty standing on the sidewalk. Dr. Campbell was there, her hands clasped over her nose and mouth.

Elaine handed the iPhone to Lila. Across the screen was a photograph of a young Black boy lying on the grass, blood oozing from his chest.

Steve was still speaking. He was saying that white people can no longer stay on the sidelines. This was not a Black problem, he yelled into the megaphone. It was a white problem. "We . . ." He spread his arms out wide to indicate the students standing around him, and then pointed to the faculty. "We cannot stay silent. We are implicated whether we do something or not. This is happening in our country. The world will implicate us. This is no time to sit in the sidelines. The time for action is now!"

Clive and Terrence exchanged glances, and then Terrence abruptly left Elaine's side. This time Elaine did not stop him. "Let's go," he said to Clive. Without a word to Lila, Clive followed him. Lila watched them leave the grounds through the campus gates.

The drummer struck the drum once, twice, and then in a frenzy of beats.

"March on!" Steve shouted. "March for justice, justice for Professor Ron Brown! Justice for that twelve-year-old boy! Black Lives Matter!"

Lila grasped Elaine's hand and, holding onto Gail with her other hand, began marching behind the students.

31

Lila had another sleepless night, and not because of nightmares of a twelve-year-old Black boy playing cops and robbers in a park. She had no siblings, but she had cousins, and cousins who had twelve-year-old sons. It would be unimaginable to them that their kid could be shot dead by the police, in a park, in a playground. But those were not her nightmares; hers were the ones Robert had caused, the shame that denied her the palliative consolation of sleep when she told him what had happened, the shame that was all-encompassing, flooding her brain, her heart, her spirit.

"Don't be so quick to jump to conclusions, Lila," Robert had remarked with a calmness that astounded her.

"The gun was fake! It was a toy gun!" she yelled back.

"The facts. Know the facts first," Robert insisted.

"What facts? Fact one, he was a child. Fact two, he was playing an imaginary game that I am certain you played as a child. Fact three—"

"Fact three," he interrupted, "you are in America."

"What are you saying?"

"I'm saying he was Black."

"And?"

"And how was the police officer to know he wouldn't try to kill him?"

Lila was aghast. "He was a kid, for God's sake!"

Robert continued unabashed: "Fact four, most of the jails in America are filled with Black men. A judge doesn't put innocent people in jail. People are in jail because they committed a crime."

Lila could not speak. She was filled with shame, for Robert, for herself, for so many people of her social class who lived on her island. Twice Robert called out her name. On the third time, the only words her brain would allow her to utter were, "He was a child. He was holding a toy. It wasn't a real gun."

"But it could have been," Robert said.

It could have been. There were other people on her island who would have said that. Cable television—CNN, MSNBC, FOX had done their job. Night after night, they beamed through their TV networks pictures that were difficult to dispute. Black men in handcuffs, Black men caught stealing from a store, Black men arraigned for mugging an old white lady, Black men charged with breaking into the homes of decent (white) people, Black men arrested for raping a white lady, Black men injecting heroin into their veins. The jails were full of them, so many Black men they had to build more jails, larger than the ones they had before. These were criminals who deserved to be caged, to be separated from decent, law-abiding (white) people. These were animals.

Fanon was right about the psychological effects of colonialism, Lila thought. But perhaps he believed colonialism would end when the colonizers went back home, to their countries in Europe, when those they had infected with their dogmas—the Black neocolonists—were too old to control the reins of power or had died.

He could not have conceived of the threat of a new colonialism, one seeping through the airwaves into the privacy of homes, children gathered around the television or peering into their iPhones.

"There are exceptions, of course," Robert was saying. "You can't paint them all with the same brush. But how are the police to know who is a criminal and who is not? I'm sure that boy was told to drop his gun."

"It wasn't a gun. It was a toy," Lila repeated through clenched teeth.

Robert was unfazed. "Like your professor, for example. Why didn't he obey the police when he was told to step away from that woman?"

Once you know, there is no unknowing. A mantra in Lila's head.

She called Terrence early the next morning. "Even if there are other witnesses, I want to make my report," she said.

"Then ask Clive to go with you."

"Why?"

"He's a lawyer."

"And that's the only reason?"

"He's a white lawyer. The police might believe you if you have a white lawyer by your side."

32

A t the precinct, the detective probed her with questions. "How far were you from the scene?" Lila said not far.

"How many feet away?"

She said she could not give him a number.

"If you were so far away, how could you see what happened?"

"I didn't say I was far away. I was close enough to see what happened."

"A few seconds ago you couldn't recall how many feet."

"I saw what I saw. Ron, Professor Brown, was giving that woman—Adriana—CPR."

"How can you be sure that was what he was doing?"

She had no evidence other than she had seen Ron pressing his hands against Adriana's chest. His mouth was on hers. Before she realized she had said those last words, the detective seized on them: "His mouth was on hers?"

"He was blowing air into her lungs."

The detective grinned. "Blowing air, huh?"

"What else would he be doing?"

Clive sat forward in his chair. "Dr. Bonnard has come here in good faith to report what she witnessed," he said.

The detective ignored him. "Did you hear when the police officer gave Professor Brown the order to move away?"

"Yes," Lila answered.

"And did you see what Professor Brown did when the police officer ordered him to move away?"

"He was trying to save Adriana. She was dying."

"But she didn't die, did she?"

"Dr. Bonnard believes that Professor Brown was trying to save Adriana's life," Clive said.

Again the detective ignored him. "Did you hear her gasping for breath?"

"She couldn't stand up," Lila said. "Her knees buckled."

"You saw all that?"

"I saw when Professor Brown helped her. She would have fallen on the pavement if he hadn't caught her."

"But she did fall, didn't she?"

"Professor Brown laid her on the ground."

"Laid her?"

Lila's mouth felt dry. She and Clive had agreed that he would come with her not as her lawyer, but as a friend. She had written out a statement. The detective had taken it but he had put it aside.

There was a pitcher of water and two glasses on the desk. The detective had placed them in front of Lila. She reached for one of the glasses. The detective poured the water for her. He waited until she had drunk most of it and had put the glass back on the table before he spoke.

"Wouldn't it have made better sense for the professor to have Adriana sit up against a wall?"

"She would be in a better position for him to give her CPR if she were lying on her back," Lila said.

"Lying on her back?"

Lila shivered.

Clive spoke again: "Dr. Bonnard has brought a statement. I don't see why that's not enough. Why the interrogation? She wants to help."

"We need objective truth here. We don't need someone who wants to help. And help who? Help the dead professor by accusing a police officer who was just doing his job? I want her to tell me what happened in her own words."

"She wrote the statement herself. Those are her own words." Clive pointed to the still-unopened envelope on the detective's desk.

"Are you a lawyer?"

"Yes, I am a lawyer," Clive said.

The detective rocked back on his chair. "Why didn't you say so at the beginning? So you see why we are so concerned about the truth. You came in here pretending—"

"But I'm not *her* lawyer," Clive said. "I'm her friend."

The detective opened the envelope. "Is it signed?"

"Yes," Clive said.

"Notarized?"

"I can do that. I'm a notary."

"So which are you? Her friend, a notary, her lawyer?"

"I'm not *her* lawyer," Clive repeated.

"We have all sorts of people coming here to report what they saw or think they saw." He shoved the envelope aside. "We have witnesses up the yazoo. Who's to believe—"

Clive locked eyes with the detective. "Dr. Bonnard has come here to tell the truth. She didn't have to come.

You have her statement. I will notarize her signature. And I am certain you will make sure that Dr. Bonnard's statement is part of the record in the case."

The detective shifted away from the steel glinting in Clive's blue eyes.

"I grew up here in Mayfield." Clive spoke again, his voice steady. "I know people. I have friends in high places. I'm sure they wouldn't want to know how you treated one of their college professors."

The detective's head jerked back. He began aimlessly shuffling papers on his desk. Clive pointed to the envelope Lila had given him. "Right," the detective said, and picked it up. "I'll see to it that Dr. Bonnard's statement gets to the right people." He stood up and shook Clive's hand.

Standing on the sidewalk outside of the police precinct, Clive did his best to reassure Lila that she had done the right thing. In her heart, she knew that was true. What troubled her, though, as she walked back to her apartment, was how correct Terrence had been, how well he understood the tensions between Black America and white America. Would she have been dismissed outright by the police if she had gone alone or if Terrence had gone with her? Would the detective have so confused her, so caused her to distrust her own testimony, that she would have become discouraged, would have torn up her written statement and have left the station?

She would have to be satisfied with not knowing the answers for certain. All she knew was that she had done the right thing.

And there was another right thing she had to do.

She looked for Steve at the cafeteria. The Black Lives Matter banner, which had been removed a few days earlier, was again stretched across the wall near the entrance of the cafeteria and there was a group of students holding posters, more of them now. Steve was not among them. Lila was disappointed but in a way she felt she had got a reprieve. She would have one more day to rehearse her apology.

She needed to return a book to the library, and after lunch she went directly there. She spotted Steve right away, sprawled out on an armchair near a window, deeply immersed in a book. He didn't hear her when she walked up to him. She cleared her throat and he looked up.

"Oh, Dr. Bonnard." He got up quickly and stretched out his hand.

It was not the greeting she was braced for and she was relieved to see the wide smile on his lips. "I don't want to disturb you," she said, shaking his hand. "I saw you and thought I'd come across and say hello."

"Want to sit down?" he asked.

"You seem pretty occupied."

"Reading," he said.

"Studying?"

"Please." He pointed to the empty armchair next to his. "You're not disturbing me at all. In fact, I'm glad to see you."

"Glad?" Lila sat down.

He joined her. "Look!" He held up the book he was reading. "Fanon."

Lila felt a rush of heat wrap around her neck. "I was wrong," she said.

"Oh, not at all. If not for you, I wouldn't be reading this."

"*Black Skin, White Masks*. It's one of your professor's favorite books."

"Yes," he said simply.

"And you're reading it? I mean, you haven't read it before?"

He crossed his legs and put down the book on the low, round table between them. "I've been wanting to talk to you," he said. "I shouldn't have lied. I hadn't read *Black Skin, White Masks*, but I knew about it. Professor Carter told me about it months ago. But I didn't know what you wanted. You were following me . . ."

"Yes," Lila admitted.

"I know why. Professor Carter told me about the note someone put under your door. That wasn't right."

"You know what the note meant?"

"Dr. Carter told me to read Fanon's book and I'd know what it meant."

"And now?"

"I haven't finished reading it, but I can tell you are not like that at all. The person who put that note under your door was a coward, a dirty, small coward."

Lila sighed. "I know who did it," she said. "And that person is not a coward. People have reasons . . ."

"Reasons to defame your reputation?"

"No one saw the note. Except the people I showed it to. My reputation was not defamed."

Steve ran his hand through his hair; the flower was exposed. Lila was amazed at the intricacy of the design. She had noticed the petals; now, close up, she could see the cup with furled edges that held the flower in place and in the center long dark lines (the *filaments*: she remembered the word from her high school botany class), each covered with a tiny fuzzy cap. It must have been painful to have that tattoo with all those tiny details inked on his tender flesh.

He followed her eyes. "It was worth the pain. I did it for my father. He was a gardener. And a pacifist," he added softly. "He served time in prison for refusing to join the army during the Vietnam War. They called him a coward. He was never able to shake off that reputation."

Lila knew little about the Vietnam War, but she knew about Muhammad Ali. He had refused to be drafted into the army. He said he couldn't shoot dark-skinned people in a country he didn't know while there were dark-skinned people hungry in America. "Just take me to jail," he said.

"Your father was not a coward," Lila said. "History has proven he was right to resist. Muhammad Ali resisted. He was a hero."

"Muhammad Ali didn't go to jail. My father went to jail."

"I'm sorry," she said.

"Don't be. My father wasn't behind bars for long. But jail taught him something. It taught him about injustice. He met a lot of Black people there. He said his white skin was what got him out of jail early."

"And yet . . ." Lila began.

"And yet I go to this privileged white college? Is that your question?"

"Something like that," Lila said.

"Because the problem of racism is a white problem,

not a Black problem. We have to fix it. We caused it; we have to right it. Here, at Mayfield, I have a chance to let white people know that."

"Why?" she asked.

"Because I profited, because my family profited from racism." He began talking about the money America made from four hundred years of free slave labor and Jim Crow; he talked about government handouts after World War II to white veterans like his grandfather; he talked about the GI Bill that gave advantages to white men; he talked about redlining in real estate.

"That's how ordinary people accumulate capital," he said. "The value of their homes increases over time, and when they sell, they're able to pass on money to their children and grandchildren. But if your home is worth nothing, because you couldn't buy a house in a decent neighborhood, you have nothing to pass on."

Then he talked about the inferior schools in Black neighborhoods, about the housing projects, about the mass incarceration of Black men, about drugs flooding into Black neighborhoods.

"You feel guilty?"

"Nah." He swiped his hand through the air. "Guilt is a waste of time and energy. I think guilt comes from selfishness, from wanting to make yourself feel better. Guilt does nothing for the other person who is suffering. I prefer to use my time and energy to act, to do something that will make a difference, something that will change the situation."

So much wisdom from someone so young. Lila remained silent.

Then, his eyes scanning the floor, Steve said softly, "I

saw you at the march." He looked up at her. "That day, on the pathway . . . what I said to you were lies."

"White lies," she said. "Inconsequential."

"White privilege. Even white lies have the benefit of being white," he said wryly.

33

The following week there was some speculation that at a trial the police officer who shot Ron Brown would be acquitted. The consensus of the more politically astute was that no juror in Mayfield was going to put a police officer, one of their own, in prison. And certainly not for killing a Black man. So the students gathered again, their numbers more than doubling, with many of the white faculty joining them. A second march was being planned. One of the leaders of the first march, a tall, thin, dark-haired teenager with intense gray eyes, was smart enough to realize that Steve had more or less taken over his role. It was Steve the students followed when he took the megaphone away from him and bellowed into it, urging the students to take a stand on the fatal shooting of a Black child, and spurring them on to demand justice for Ron Brown. This second march would go beyond the campus into the village of Mayfield, Steve announced. He passed out flyers giving the time and place. In bold print, in the center of the flyer, he repeated his call to arms: *We cannot stay silent! The time for action is now!*

Then, just before dawn, on the day the march was supposed to take place, the snow began to fall.

Mrs. Lowell had warned Lila that winter comes fast and early in Vermont. When Lila arrived at her office, the snowflakes were falling intermittently and melted as soon as they hit the grass, but by midmorning, when the march was to begin, the snow had thickened and not even the slightest hint of green remained on the lawn. From her office window Lila could see the few students who had gathered early around the flagpole, at the circle opposite to the library, returning reluctantly to the academic building. It was evident that the march would have to be canceled. Hills of snow had begun to accumulate on empty benches. It was the winter wonderland Lila had read about and she was eager to take photos to send to Robert.

Clive came to her office to give her the news that the march was postponed and Lila convinced him to go outside with her. "Robert wouldn't believe how beautiful it is," she said.

"Pretty, but very cold," Clive said. "You'll have to wrap up."

Lila put on her coat, gloves, and wool hat, and wrapped her scarf around her neck. Clive pointed to her boots. They were too fancy for the snow, he told her. "You need waterproof boots," he said.

"Wellingtons?"

He grinned. "I guess that's what the British call them."

She smiled back and looked out of the window. "It's like a transparent curtain of white jewels out there."

"You should see it in December," Clive said.

"I may be gone in December."

"*May?*"

She had promised Robert to be home for Christmas. And yet now there were lies and secrets between them.

He had lied to her grandmother; she had lied to him. Not directly. Her lie was one of omission. She had allowed him to believe she would not go to the police. She had told him about the march, but not that she had joined the marchers. And there was the shame she'd felt when he discredited the account of that child's death. But she had given him her word.

"I will be gone for almost all of December," she corrected herself.

Clive zipped up his jacket and dropped the subject. "Okay," he said, "let's go outside. Only to the top step. I'll catch you if you slip."

The custodians had already begun clearing the snow from the entrance of the academic building, but as fast as they shoveled, the snow kept blanketing the front steps. Clive slid his hand under Lila's elbow. "Careful," he said.

Lila took pictures, fewer than she intended, conscious of the light pressure of Clive's hand on her arm. Part of her wanted to ask him to remove his hand. He was making it difficult to hold the iPhone in place to take the photographs. And yet she liked his hand there. She told herself that she liked it because he would hold her if she slipped. That was partially true, but not completely.

They didn't stay long outside. The snow was now falling in fat bundles and they decided to return to her office. No sooner had they arrived when her phone pinged; it was the president of the college announcing the cancelation of classes for the rest of the day.

"Come, I'll walk you home," Clive offered.

Lila didn't respond and Clive stood silently while

she gathered the papers on her desk and put them into her briefcase.

"A penny for your thoughts," Clive said.

"I was thinking of home," she confessed.

"It must be warm there."

"No snow," she said, laughing.

"Do you miss it?"

"The sea, the sun, the green grass."

"You have regrets? Coming here?"

"Oh, no. None at all," she said quickly. "I've learned a lot." She reached for a book on her desk.

"I can wait until you're ready to leave," he said.

"No need." She put the book back down and shut her briefcase. "I'm ready. I have all the papers I need."

On the way to Mrs. Lowell's, Clive said, "America can sometimes be an ugly place. That little boy . . . Terrence went with me to Brooklyn. Lawyers from my firm offered to defend the kid the police shot. Pro bono."

"They would do that?" Neither he nor Terrence had said a word to her about their sudden departure at the beginning of the last march, and though she was curious, she had not probed.

"Of course, win or lose we can go to court, mount a civil case. Make the city pay, so we won't lose financially." A deep sadness clouded his eyes. "It's a blot on our country, the racism here. The police see a Black man, even a Black boy, and all they see is a Black body. They shoot first and ask questions later."

A Black body. Terrence had used the same words. Lila tightened the scarf around her neck. "Why didn't you say anything?"

"I assumed Terrence told you. I was waiting for you to bring it up."

They walked in silence, Lila needing the quiet and stillness to make sense of Terrence's reluctance to tell her that he had asked for Clive's help, his firm's help, in getting justice for the killing of the young boy.

Robert's solution to racism was intermarriage. "Like we have in the Caribbean. Everybody is mixed up. Not a family who doesn't have a relative who doesn't look like them, someone who has African blood, or is Indian, or Chinese, or white. And I don't mean a distant relative, I mean a first cousin. You can't have racism if your aunty or your uncle or your granny or your grandpa doesn't look like you. How are you going to be prejudiced against them?"

Once Lila had shared that view. But she had also known another truth. When she was in high school, there were two girls who had the same surname. One was very dark-skinned, her hair cut in a tightly curled Afro; the other was white, or appeared to be white. She was blond, with light gray-blue eyes. Lila was best friends with the blond girl. It was only when she was at university that she learned that the girls were first cousins. Neither had acknowledged the other.

Terrence had opened her eyes to a deeper understanding of racism. It was observable in differences in skin color, but its true insidiousness lay in the ugly and persistent current of lies, too often accepted as fact: one race was superior to the other; one more human than the other. Did her blond friend think she was superior to her dark-skinned cousin? Did she fear she would be tainted by association if everyone knew they shared the same blood?

They had reached Mrs. Lowell's house and the snow hadn't abated. Clive was wearing a hat but not a scarf and seemed unaffected by the flakes of snow that brushed his bare neck. Lila was shivering; she pulled her scarf over her nose and mouth.

"I can barely see you," Clive said, teasing her.

"I don't know how you can stand it. I'm freezing, though I must admit it's beautiful."

"That it is," he said.

Someone was clearing the snow off the steps to Mrs. Lowell's front door. "I can make it safely inside from here," Lila said, and stuck out her hand. "Thanks for walking me home."

Clive took her hand, but he did not shake it. He clasped it between his two palms. "Must you go back in December?"

Lila pulled her hand away. "I have to go."

She looked back when she reached the front door. He was still standing by the gate, snow falling all around him, the top of his coat dusted white, his skimpy knit hat barely protecting his head. She waved and he waved back. He was still standing there when she closed the door behind her.

34

The march was canceled because of the heavy snow, but a sudden wave of warm weather melted what remained after the snowplows had cleared the streets, and so there was nothing to prevent another march. It was no longer an unfounded rumor that the police officer who killed Ron Brown would likely be acquitted. Some big-name lawyers had been hired to defend him. No one knew for certain who had put up the money for the lawyers, but it was well known that there were two billionaire brothers, rabid supporters of the Second Amendment, the right of citizens to bear arms, who had taken a special interest in the case. *The only thing that stops a bad guy with a gun is a good guy with a gun*—this was one of their most popular slogans. The police officer swore (and there were witnesses from the town who corroborated his account) that Ron had reached into his pocket and pulled out something that any reasonable person would conclude was a gun. He had to shoot Ron before Ron shot him. The decision of his commanding officer was fair: the police officer was reassigned to another precinct and given the full protection of the law.

The news that some high-powered lawyers who had never lost a case had been hired to defend the police officer appeared in a small column on the front page of the

Mayfield newspaper, but it made the headlines in the student paper. This time, as the students had planned previously, the march began at the college but continued through the streets of Mayfield. A few townspeople joined in, following the students solemnly in a tight row in the back, not uttering a word nor turning to greet neighbors who waved at them. None of them carried placards; the students did, signs that read, *Black Lives Matter*, *A Black Child Matters*, *Justice for Ron Brown*, and drummers pounded to the rhythm of the students' chants. Eventually the march wound its way without incident back to the end of Main Street, just outside the campus. The crowd dispersed and the police in squad cars and on foot returned to their usual duties.

"That's it?" Lila asked, incredulous. She was standing on the sidewalk next to Elaine, Gail, and Terrence, shocked that the streets had emptied so quickly. Now there were people strolling arm in arm, talking and laughing, teenagers jostling each other, children playing tag, restaurants opening their doors to happy diners, stores welcoming customers.

"For this town, what just happened on their main road is historic," Terrence said.

"And will there be another march?" Lila asked.

"Only if there's another killing," Elaine said bitterly.

"If that cop is in fact acquitted, there'll be appeals," said Gail.

"Useless appeals." Elaine sniffed, then reached into handbag and took out a tissue. "The students will go home for Christmas break." She wiped her eyes and blew her nose. "They will drink, eat, and be merry, and when they come back, they'll forget about this. 'History is written by the winners.' That's what they say. They know that sad truth all right. We aren't the winners here. Our history will be distorted. They'll find some excuse to explain Ron's murder, that child's murder, the murder of more innocent Black men . . ."

Terrence put his arm around her. "It's not over, Elaine. We have good lawyers too. And Clive will get his firm in Brooklyn to help."

"What can Clive do? What can anyone do?"

"Come, Elaine." Gail took her hand. "Let me drive you home. Will you be okay, Lila?"

"It's a short walk for me," Lila said. "Anyhow, I have to get a book I forgot in my office."

"Terrence will go with you. Won't you, Terrence?"

"Of course," he said.

At the college's parking lot, after Gail and Elaine had driven away, Lila put her hand on Terrence's arm and confronted him with the question that had continued to trouble her: "Why didn't you tell me about the boy?"

"The boy the police killed?"

"You didn't say anything."

"What's more to say? You heard what they said on TV. He had a toy gun, and the police killed him."

"I know. What I don't know is what you and Clive found out when you went to Brooklyn. Why didn't you tell me? "

Terrence scraped his shoes against the ground.

"You still don't trust me. Is that it?"

"I trust you, Lila, but as I've told you before, it's our fight."

"And mine too," she said.

He smiled, but he didn't respond.

His smile was warning enough for Lila. He was shutting her out, but this time his refusal to admit her into his confidence did not hurt as much. He had said he trusted her. And perhaps that was as much as she could ask for.

They went to her office to get the book she had left there and afterward Terrence walked with her to Mrs. Lowell's. She invited him inside for a cup of tea but he declined.

"I have an appointment," he said.

"A date?"

He winked.

"Someone in Mayfield?" she asked.

"Not in Mayfield. I'm not like Ron."

"That's not fair," she admonished, sensing immediately what he was insinuating.

He threw up his hands. "What can I say? I love Black women."

"And didn't Ron?"

"If he hadn't gotten mixed up . . ."

"So you're blaming him?"

"No. Not at all. Absolutely not at all. I'm blaming the police officers who killed him. I'm blaming this country that stays silent when Black men become prey."

"What about the students? They didn't stay silent."

"They're our hope," Terrence said. "We're counting on the young generation. But Ron should have known better. He made himself an easy target."

"A target?"

"Dating Adriana."

"Your date? I suppose she's a Black woman?"

"Beautiful inside and out."

"And where did you meet her?"

"In Brooklyn. At a protest march a couple of months ago. We're meeting up in Bloomington. Did the e-mail thing for a while, but now we're getting closer."

"A long-distance romance?"

"I doubt she'd come to Mayfield."

"And what will you do, move to Brooklyn?"

"Everything's happening in Brooklyn these days," he said. "It's the place to be. Center of the universe." He winked again and then added more soberly, "If Black people can hold on to their houses . . . But money talks. Gentrification, you know."

35

Mrs. Lowell opened the door before Lila could put the key in the lock. She was wringing her hands and looking anxiously over Lila's shoulders up and down the sidewalk. "Come in. Come in," she beckoned. Lila stepped inside and Mrs. Lowell quickly closed the door behind her. "I don't want trouble."

"Trouble?" Lila asked.

"Look at what happened to that man."

"Dr. Brown." Lila tried to suppress the flash of anger that burned her chest. But at least Mrs. Lowell had acknowledged it wasn't a student or a car accident.

"I didn't say anything, but I didn't think it was a good idea for you to go to the march. And now Dr. Campbell is trying to reach you. She called twice. She said it's very important for you to call her back."

"Twice? Did she say why?"

"You are a grown woman and you can make your own decisions, but I didn't think it was a good idea. Not at all. All kinds of trouble happen in situations like that. Those protest marches, they just stir up trouble."

Lila did her best to convey to Mrs. Lowell that the march was peaceful. Nobody was hurt. Everyone left safely when it ended.

Mrs. Lowell shook her head. Marches are dangerous,

she said. Not military ones. She likes military marches. Political ones just cause trouble. There is a better way to settle disputes. There's the law, there are courts. Justice is blind; it's fair, she said.

Lila did not argue with her. Mrs. Lowell belonged to another age, another time. Her interactions with Black people were limited to those she had hired to serve her: the woman who cleaned her house, whom she professed to love (she gave her gifts for her children every Christmas), and the mechanic who had fixed her husband's car when her husband was alive. Those were good people, Mrs. Lowell said. The Black people in jail are bad people; they are criminals. It had never occurred to her to question whether the justice she so admired was also applied to them.

Yet even after Lila reassured her again, Mrs. Lowell repeated her fears. She had wanted to warn Lila about going to the march, but . . .

Lila was worried too. She had seen Dr. Campbell at the previous march and she remembered her reaction to the news about the twelve-year-old boy. Dr. Campbell seemed shocked, upset. But did she blame the boy's parents, as some had? Did she believe that the police officer who gunned down the child was innocent? Did she think Ron was responsible for forcing that police officer's hand? Lila shuddered at the thought. And, like Mrs. Lowell, did Dr. Campbell also disapprove of her participation in the march?

Terrence had warned her. Be careful, he said. And more and more Lila was noticing that there was increasing talk on the radio and television about closing America's borders. Too many immigrants, conservative pundits claimed. Soon white people, the rightful citizens of America, would find themselves in a minority, replaced by a marauding horde. Immigrants had been apprehended for murder, rape, theft.

Could the police make the same mistake as they had with Ron and take her for a criminal?

Once inside her room, Lila called Dr. Campbell. Her fears could not have been more misplaced. Dr. Campbell greeted her warmly. She had some news that she wanted to deliver personally. Was Lila free for dinner the following evening? Lila was, and they arranged to meet at a restaurant. Dr. Campbell knew the chef there and promised that the food would be delicious.

And the meal was indeed excellent. Expensive too: shrimp cocktail, an exotic salad, stuffed lobster tails, baked potatoes, asparagus. Dr. Campbell ordered a bottle of fine white wine. She kept Lila in suspense until the dessert was served and then, raising her glass, she shared her news.

The president of the college had agreed with her recommendation to offer Lila a contract for another year at Mayfield. "You don't have to give me your answer now," Dr. Campbell said. "I expect you'll have to discuss this with your family back home."

"With my fiancé," Lila said. "He's expecting me to return."

"The president means to make you an attractive offer. He'll include a travel budget so you can go home during the school breaks. This is a great opportunity for you, Lila."

Lila forced herself to smile. "Please tell the president that I'm grateful."

Dr. Campbell blinked and her face darkened. Clearly, this was not the enthusiastic response she was expecting. "A whole year, Lila. A generous salary! I know with the exchange of US dollars . . ."

"Yes, it'll be more than twice the salary I get at my university."

"So you'll say yes?"

"I don't want to disappoint you."

"What is it?" Dr. Campbell pressed her. "Are you unhappy here? Is that it?"

"Oh, no," Lila responded quickly. "Everyone has been kind. I love my students."

"So I can tell the president that you'll consider his offer?"

"My grandmother," Lila said. "She's not young and she'll need me."

"As I said, there'll be Christmas break, spring break. Your travel paid for."

"It's really a very generous offer," Lila said. She thanked Dr. Campbell again.

"Your grandmother has other grandchildren, doesn't she?"

"Yes, I do have cousins."

"I know this comes suddenly, but we would be really pleased to have you for another year. The president, me, all of Mayfield College. We all want you to stay. So you'll give the president's offer some thought?"

"I promise," Lila said, but she already knew her answer.

The next morning Terrence appeared at her doorway. She had just returned to her office after teaching her first class. She waved him in. He was grinning from ear to ear. "So?" he said, approaching her.

Lila stood up. "So, what?"

"So another year, huh?"

Lila sat back down and asked him to close the door behind him.

"An appointment for another year! Wow!"

"How'd you know?"

"President to president. Though, of course, I'm a faux president. Now that Ron is gone, the president thinks I'm the leader of our tiny group of Black faculty. I don't think he would have given me any thought except he doesn't like the press. There was a photograph in the newspaper. Did you see it?"

Lila hadn't.

"I should have brought the paper for you. It wasn't on the front page. Somewhere buried inside, on page seven or so. A picture of the Black Lives Matter march through Mayfield, with a short paragraph, but it was enough to scare the administration. What might come next? What will happen when the trial begins? People could start accusing Mayfield College of racism." Terrence sneered. "Good old Mayfield College, imagine that! But the president saw some of the townspeople marching with the students yesterday. Apparently they were asking questions: Why are there so few Black students at Mayfield? How many Black faculty has he hired? I don't know who complained, but the president called me this morning and said he was going to make a change. He plans to begin with you."

"I'm not interested," Lila said flatly, and leaned back in her chair.

"Not interested?" Terrence stared at her. "What do you mean? This is what I predicted. I knew they'd want you to stay."

"I'm not staying."

"Why? Because of your fiancé? If he loves you, he'll wait."

"Maybe."

"Then what else? What's holding you back from accepting the offer? I understand it's a generous one."

"I think the president should hire an African American," Lila said quietly.

"Whoa!" Terrence sank into an armchair in front of Lila's desk. "Whoa!" he repeated. "Is that you speaking, Lila?"

"Are you surprised?"

"I don't know what to say."

"You opened my eyes."

"Lila, Lila." Terrence pulled at his right earlobe and grinned bashfully.

"It's true," Lila said.

"So what are you going to do?"

"Go back home. I don't want to be a token for anybody, for any cause. If I accept this offer, I'll be easing consciences, the president's and the town's. I'll be good for the college's statistics. They'll be able to add me to your three, a replacement for Ron. Then next they'll talk about how exceptional I am, how brilliant. But there are hundreds like me, thousands of Black women. Black women who far surpass me in intelligence and scholarship. The president can find one of those women here, in America, even in your state. He doesn't have to re-cross the Atlantic."

Terrence could not stop grinning. "Recross the Atlantic? That's a good one."

"They came to get us as slave labor for the plantations. Now they're back for us to clean up their mess. I won't be complicit in an attempt to whitewash racism."

Terrence slapped his knees and laughed out loud, mirthlessly. "Whitewash racism!! You're on a roll, Lila."

"I'm serious."

Terrence straightened up and furrowed his brow. "I know you are, Lila, I know you are."

"There's more. I suspect white America is more comfortable with us, foreign Blacks. With you, African Americans, they have a constant reminder of America's original sin. With us, there's no connection, at least not in America."

Terrence stood up and reached for her hand. "I applaud you, Lila."

Shaking his hand, Lila replied soberly, "No need."

He had to leave—his class was about to begin—but just as his fingers touched the doorknob, he turned back. "So not the same Lila, huh?" He wrinkled his brow.

"A more informed Lila," she said.

He exhaled. "Thank you."

"For what?"

"For understanding."

36

When Lila told Robert about the job offer, he said, "You have to come back home."

It was his tone that offended her: he was ordering her to return to the island.

"You have responsibilities," he said. "You have duties to the university here. Obligations. They gave you a year off, but they expect you to return. There are students waiting for you. You can't stay. You *have* to turn down their offer. And your grandmother. It's unfair to leave her for another year."

Had he not mentioned her grandmother, he might not have cemented a thought growing in the recesses of her mind. "Mrs. Lowell," she said.

"What about her?"

"She needs me too."

"What are you saying, Lila? You want to stay for another year for Mrs. Lowell? Is *that* what you're saying? Mrs. Lowell is your landlady, for God's sake."

"I'm thinking of spending Christmas here. To be with her. My grandmother has grandchildren. My cousins will be with her. Mrs. Lowell is a widow; she has no children. She'll be alone at Christmas."

Lila could hear him literally chewing his lower lip. He was angry with her but he was forcing himself to control his emotions. He would not beg. He would be cool, rational.

"So you've made up your mind?"

She hadn't until that moment. "Yes. I'll spend Christmas here, in Mayfield, with Mrs. Lowell. But I'll come back home at the end of my contract in June."

"You know what you're telling me?"

"Yes."

"And our plans for Christmas?"

"Mrs. Lowell will be lonely," she said.

"And me? What about me?"

"Too much has changed, Robert."

"I haven't changed. I'm the same Robert you left behind when you went to America."

"That's the problem. *I've* changed. I don't see the world as you do."

"Is this about that professor who was shot?"

"Yes."

"And that boy?"

"That too."

"You aren't thinking of joining some Black Power movement, are you, Lila? Don't let them infect you with their resentments."

"It's not about resentments. It's about righting a wrong that people have been forced to suffer for hundreds of years. It's about justice."

"And you plan to join them?"

She was silent.

"Don't go turning into some Black Power radical, Lila."

"I'm coming back home, Robert. At the end of the school year, I'll be back for good."

"But not for me?"

She did not have the heart nor the courage to answer him.

"There's another man, isn't there?"

"No other man," she said.

"And this is what you want?"

"It's what I want."

37

There was no other man, but there was Clive. Clive was a friend. She had not so much as kissed him on the cheek. He had kissed her hand; that was it. Yet it bothered her now that she had not told Robert of the times she had tea with Clive, or the times Clive had come to her office. Of course, she couldn't tell him that he went with her to the police precinct since Robert didn't know she hadn't followed his advice. His demands.

Mrs. Lowell was a ruse, made up on the spot when Robert tried to manipulate her with guilt. It was true she was expected to return to her university after her year at Mayfield, but Lila had no doubt that if she wanted to stay, the chair of her department would grant her an additional year's leave. Plus, there would be more money for the department if the university did not have to pay her salary for a year. No, none of the reasons Robert gave her had dissuaded her. She had declined the offer from Mayfield for the reasons she told Terrence.

In the end, the president was not unhappy with her decision. The specter of marauding Black Lives Matter protesters that had terrified him turned out to be unfounded. There was no trial; the lawyers hired by the two billionaire bothers had managed to convince the mayor and the attorney general that a trial would not be good for the small town of Mayfield. A trial would tarnish their Disney World image. All the bad press, the marches through the streets, the Black Lives Matter placards everywhere! It would take years for Mayfield to recover. Better to offer Ron Brown's family a generous settlement, one they would accept, and then transfer the cops to another town where nobody would know them. People have short memories, the lawyers argued. Soon they'll forget.

And so it was that by early December, Mayfield was decked out for the holidays, memories of the killing on Main Street all but faded. A huge pine Christmas tree was installed in the center of the park, decorated with white lights and shiny gold banners looped over the branches and delicate white angels with silvery wings hanging down from thin white ribbons. Shop owners were busy stringing multicolored Christmas lights across their buildings and putting up big red bows on windows and Christmas wreaths on doors. The cheerful voices of practicing carol singers could be heard streaming from churches and schools and Christmas music was piped out of the entrance of the town hall.

Clive called to say he was coming back to Mayfield for Christmas. He sounded happy. "Negotiations on the settlement are going well," he told Lila. "Better than I expected. The town claims it's broke, but we're going after the state. There's money in the state."

"So you've given up on a trial?" Lila said.

"There are people who swear they saw a gun in Ron's hand. Or something like a gun."

"But you told me there were witnesses who said the opposite."

"Not enough of them."

"What about my statement? The evidence I gave the police."

"They are from Mayfield, the people who claimed Robert had a gun. They live here."

"You mean they are white," Lila said quietly.

Clive sighed. "It would be an uphill battle, Lila. Cops have immunity. *Qualified* immunity. It's supposed to protect them from charges if what they did was, so to speak, done on the job."

"Even if they killed someone?"

"*Especially* if they killed someone. And especially if the someone they killed was Black," Clive said.

Lila was silent on the phone.

"I don't mean to depress you," Clive said quickly. "There'll be lots of money in the settlement Ron's family will get. Money can't make up for a human life. That cop—those cops should pay for the life they took. That would be justice. They should pay for taking away all the dreams Ron had for himself, the years he spent preparing for that future, the sacrifices he had to make, his PhD, his scholarship, the students he would have influenced. Ron would have made a mark on the world. But Ron will leave a legacy. He had siblings, two still in college. The money will pay for their education; it'll give them a good start in life. There are other relatives who won't have to worry about paying for college. And the truth is, a legacy is as much as we can hope for after we leave this earth. A good legacy, that is."

"What's this about leaving the earth?" Lila asked jokingly in an attempt to break the soberness of his tone. "You have years ahead of you."

"Just a reality check. I wouldn't want to leave this earth when you're on it."

Lila felt her neck grow hot and her heart bounded. She was glad they were on the phone and he couldn't see the smile plastered across her face or hear the thumping in her chest.

"So what are you doing for dinner tonight?" he asked.

"No plans," she said.

"Then have dinner with me . . . The same restaurant?"

"Yes, the food there was great."

"And the company, I hope."

"And the company," she conceded.

There was a Christmas tree in the restaurant too. It gave the dining room a refreshing outdoorsy smell. Lila inhaled deeply. "It's lovely in here," she said, exhaling.

Clive looked pleased. "Mayfield puts on a show at Christmastime. There'll be a concert in the town hall and carol singing."

The waiter came and Clive chose the wine. It was an expensive selection and Lila objected. "Just this once. For Christmas," Clive said, and the waiter poured some wine into Lila's glass and then into his. "To you, Lila." Clive raised his glass. "Much happiness."

"And to you too," Lila replied.

Clive pointed to the clutch of poinsettias at the bottom of the Christmas tree. "There'll be poinsettias in almost all the shop windows, stuffed in pots wrapped with all colors of foil. There'll be red, white, pink poinsettias." He paused. "I know they're not the same as the ones you have on your island."

"We have trees. Poinsettia trees. They bloom at Christmas."

"Ours are dwarfs. We force them to bloom."

"Back home, poinsettia trees grow wild against fences."

Clive sucked in his breath, exhaled, and his chest deflated. "So I suppose there's no way to persuade you to stay? Even for the holidays?"

"I'm not going."

Perhaps she had spoken too softly, or perhaps he had despaired of persuading her, for he didn't respond. He swirled the wine in his glass and brought it to his lips.

"I decided," she said. "Mrs. Lowell . . ."

And like an echo rebounding in his ear, he heard her at last. "Not going? You'll stay?"

"Yes. I'll get to see your town all dressed up on Christmas Day."

"Your fiancé?"

She splayed her fingers. "No ring."

"I didn't—"

"It's over," she said.

He reached for her hand. For a long time she let him hold it.

Author's Note

Friends have asked me why I chose to highlight William Melvin Kelley's *A Different Drummer* in this novel. I hope my reasons are evident. But I want to add that Kelley's life and work are a cautionary tale for our times about the possibility of reversals in spite of the recent passionate outcry of millions in America and across the world demanding racial justice.

A Different Drummer was Kelley's first novel. It was published in 1962 when the author was merely twenty-four. For a Black man, Kelley had lived a charmed life. His father was an editor of the *Amsterdam News*, the oldest and most widely circulated Black newspaper in the country. From first grade through high school, Kelley went to Fieldston, a prestigious largely white prep school where he achieved high grades in most of his classes. After Fieldston, Kelley was accepted into Harvard but left one semester shy of graduating. Nevertheless, while he was at Harvard, he won the Dana Reed Prize for creative writing by a Harvard undergraduate. One of his mentors was the famous modernist poet Archibald MacLeish.

According to the *New Yorker*, *A Different Drummer* received high critical praise and seemed to herald the start of a brilliant career for Kelley. He went on whirlwind tours across the country to give readings of the novel and was invited to present lectures at some of America's most distinguished institutions. Kelley published three more novels, but by the third, he was no longer a literary star. He was only thirty-two then, and for the rest of his life, though he continued to write diligently, he was never published again. In his seventies, Kelley was seen at night in the back alleys of restaurants in Harlem searching for food in garbage cans. His wife, Aiki Kelley, attributed the downturn in Kelley's fortunes to the changing political climate in America; she believed that her husband was a casualty of the decline of the Civil Rights Movement in the late sixties and early seventies. As the momentum ebbed, she said, "those with the power to make publishing decisions turned their attention elsewhere."

Acknowledgments

My thanks to Johnny Temple, the amazing publisher of Akashic Books. His editorial feedback on this novel was invaluable. My thanks also to my agent Malaika Adero for her editorial advice at a crucial stage in the revision process. As always, I am thankful for the loving support of my son, Jason Harrell, and his family: his wife, Denise, and my two granddaughters, Jordan and Savannah. COVID, in a strange way, brought my close-knit family even closer together. The daily texts from my five brothers and five sisters and the frequent long telephone conversations brought immense joy to my life and made writing this novel possible. My thanks and love to all of them.